MARGUERITE, CALVIN & RABELAIS

MARGUERITE, CALVIN & RABELAIS

A Humanist Tale of Three Democrats 1529-1534

GARY ARTHUR THOMSON

iUniverse

MARGUERITE, CALVIN & RABELAIS
A HUMANIST TALE OF THREE DEMOCRATS 1529-1534

Copyright © 2017 Gary Arthur Thomson.

All rights reserved. No part of this book may be used or reproduced by any means, graphic, electronic, or mechanical, including photocopying, recording, taping or by any information storage retrieval system without the written permission of the author except in the case of brief quotations embodied in critical articles and reviews.

This is a work of fiction. All of the characters, names, incidents, organizations, and dialogue in this novel are either the products of the author's imagination or are used fictitiously.

iUniverse books may be ordered through booksellers or by contacting:

iUniverse
1663 Liberty Drive
Bloomington, IN 47403
www.iuniverse.com
1-800-Authors (1-800-288-4677)

Because of the dynamic nature of the Internet, any web addresses or links contained in this book may have changed since publication and may no longer be valid. The views expressed in this work are solely those of the author and do not necessarily reflect the views of the publisher, and the publisher hereby disclaims any responsibility for them.

Any people depicted in stock imagery provided by Thinkstock are models, and such images are being used for illustrative purposes only.
Certain stock imagery © Thinkstock.

ISBN: 978-1-5320-2110-7 (sc)
ISBN: 978-1-5320-2112-1 (hc)
ISBN: 978-1-5320-2111-4 (e)

Library of Congress Control Number: 2017907715

Print information available on the last page.

iUniverse rev. date: 05/13/2017

dedicated to Jeanette, my wife

Our Website: iOriginsBooks.com

Foreword

This historical novel is about a slice of history 1529-1534 in France. The people are all in their twenties and thirties—Marguerite, Francis I, Calvin, Rabelais, Renée and Marot. They are full of hopes and dreams about the future. It is the high moment of the Renaissance—the rebirth of humanism after a thousand years of feudal Dark Ages. They talk. They sing folk tunes and dance the gavotte. They ride spirited white ponies. They build well-designed houses and gardens.

The five years of this novel were a brief moment of hope. After that, the Inquisition murdered half the population of France or forced them to flee to places like Québec. So this novel does not reflect these people in their fifties when their hopes had been destroyed. This novel is a slice of history where young people have great expectations and hope is alive.

They met at Bourges Law College...

The rear wheel swerved. The carriage careened into the ditch. From his lofty driver's seat, Guy catapulted on eagle's wings and then descended into a prickly thicket. Squawking birds, buzzing bees and a lone wild boar burst out of the underbrush. The four driverless horses jerked to and fro constrained by their harness.

Luc, on the lead mount, rode a few paces ahead. He reared his steed and raced back. Grabbing the nearest bridal bit, Luc pulled the horses into line. Dismounting, he spoke quietly and gently stroked their necks. They knew his familiar voice from the stable where he brushed them down and fed them.

Queen Marguerite was riding her white stallion accompanied by her horseman, Jean Pierre. Horror-struck, they watched the royal box lurch and come to rest in a tilt—the door facing skyward. The calamity dissolved into stunned silence...

Swiftly Queen Marguerite and Jean Pierre dismounted. He wrenched the door open. Lassie, the Queen's Border collie, jumped out and raced around in a state of nervous confusion.

"Are you okay Heléne?" Jean Pierre shouted to the Queen's handmaid inside. Heléne was his wife.

"I'm okay," came a faint voice from the interior of the compartment. Heléne had been lying on the passenger seat. The leather cushioned walls and ceiling had protected her like pillows.

Jean Pierre heisted himself up and threw a leg over the

threshold of the door. Then he climbed down inside the cab to assist his wife up and out. Holding the reins of the two stallions, Marguerite watched the two climb out of the cab.

"Heléne! Are you sure that you are all right?" she asked her handmaid.

"I am indeed, M'lady," Heléne's face appeared.

"Are you bruised?"

"Not so far as I can see? The seat cushions protected me."

"Thank goodness for that."

"Where did the dog go?" asked Jean Pierre.

"Lassie is here with me," Luc blurted. He was grooming the horses with a currycomb to calm them down.

"Maybe you should unhitch the horses," put forth Jean Pierre. "Walk them about a bit. This will take some time to fix."

Guy, the driver, extricated himself from the roadside thicket. He came around with bloody cuts and scratches from the prickly undergrowth. He brushed leaves and debris off his coat.

"You're a sight for sore eyes," Marguerite said sympathetically.

"No bother, M'lady," Guy mumbled appreciatively.

"I heard a wild boar squeal when you fell," Jean Pierre noted. "Maybe there are truffles?"

"At the moist base of old trees," Heléne picked up, "wild boars root up truffles."

Heléne looked at her son, Luc. "Let's go look for truffles while they fix the wheel. Fleshy mushrooms will be a real delicacy at our table."

Putting her hands on Heléne and Guy, Marguerite drew her people together. "I'm glad no one is hurt," she said. "We've escaped injury."

The little group nodded appreciatively awaiting her instructions.

"I think I will ride on to Bourges," Marguerite asserted directing her eyes at Jean Pierre.

"Will you be safe? One of us can ride with you," he responded.

"It's only a couple of miles. We can already see the towers and pinnacles of the cathedral. But thanks for your concern."

As the Queen's overseer, Jean Pierre took control, "Guy and I will fix the wheel. Heléne and Luc will gather truffles. Then we'll follow you to Bourges."

"Take the horses and carriage to the royal livery," Marguerite proffered. "Then enjoy your evening at the royal arms."

Then she mounted and rode off in a cloud of dust. Lassie followed in hot pursuit.

Queen Marguerite of Navarre had been in residing at Clos Lucé, a petite chateau where Leonardo da Vinci had lived his last five years. The chateau stood in the shadow of the great royal residence at Amboise overlooking the Loire River.

Chateau Clos Lucé was a quiet place where Marguerite was able to think alone. At the side of the Grande Salon in the upper rooms, a bay window provided Marguerite a small niche for a chair and desk to write. She looked out on the well-tended gardens behind the chateau. A contraption that Leonardo invented lifted water to irrigate the plots of flowers, vegetables and herbs. A stable and coach barn concealed the rear wall.

Jean Pierre, Heléne, Luc and Guy were all posted at Clos Lucé as caretakers. They worked and lived in the lower quarters. Heléne prepared nutritious cuisine upstairs and down. The men maintained the chateau, the grounds and gardens, the coaches and the stable.

Today the four accompanied her to Bourges. To a bystander watching the scene, the Queen's entourage formed a parade of sorts. A lone horseman taking the lead. Four horses drawing the royal carriage. Bringing up the rear on two magnificent white stallions, the Queen riding alongside her horseman.

Then the roadside accident occurred…

Queen Marguerite galloped into Bourges—the strong three-beat gait of her horse clattered her arrival on the cobblestone street. Like a drum major, her well-groomed collie took the lead.

Queen Marguerite, Duchess of Berry, sat astraddle her horse dressed in Gaelic *triubhas*. Her shapely trousered-legs flanked her white stallion. She looked quite smart in her equestrian attire. Marguerite could thank her predecessor, Queen Margaret of Scotland, wife of Louis XI, for this *'LEG-acy'* of the *'auld alliance.'* Skirted English women sat superciliously and unsafely sidesaddle. The Scottish precedent that Queen Margaret had set was to sit *'astride'* not *'aside'* her equine *'horsie'*.

Marguerite had been raised on the royal estate at Cognac near Angoulême. Stone fences circled vast fields and pastures. Flowered meadows fitted into dark forests. In these environs, she grew up riding horses. She raced with her brother Francis over hills and dales.

Queen Marguerite's mother, Louise of Savoy was widowed on New Year's Day 1496. Marguerite was four and Francis two when their father, Charles of Angoulême died. Louise was grateful for the security of her provincial home at Cognac.

Charles had cultivated a library of well-chosen books. Louise encouraged the education of her children. From their birth, they were reading stories and singing chansons together. Soon they were acting out stories and musicals. A writer herself, Louise encouraged her children to take up the quill and keep journals.

Slowing her steed to a frisky walk, Queen Marguerite rode into the university commons. Students were milling about—one-upping each other in adolescent undergraduate banter.

"Look there, a woman is riding a horse into the cloisters," a visiting Oxford don jeered somewhat disapprovingly.

"She's wearing a man's riding togs at that," quipped a second Cambridge don who quickly feigned looking away aghast.

"Pardon Sirs," said an undergraduate, "but she is the Queen." The undaunted dons had no comment.

"She is not without precedent," stated the Chancellor who had overheard the visiting English dons, "Queen Margaret, wife of Louis XI who founded this university, wore such attire. In the Gallic tongue, they are called *triubhas*. Margaret played tennis wearing tight-legged trousers in these very commons!"

Looking smartly in her riding habit, Queen Marguerite dismounted from her horse and nodded to the Chancellor. Then she handed the reins to one of the very dons who had been so disdainful and disapproving.

"Would you kindly take my horse to the royal stables?" And without waiting for a response from the stupefied don, she entered the Chamber of Law built by Louis the Eleventh.

The Chancellor chuckled and followed her in.

The disabled barouche box consisted of a narrow set of front wheels and a wider pair of rear wheels. In between, chains attached to springs suspended the passenger box. One of the wider-tracking rear wheels had caught a sharp rock as they moved through a rutted narrows in the roadway. The metal rim had come off and a spoke in the wooden wheel had been broken.

Jean Pierre quickly took charge. Guy began building a ring of fire under the heavy metal rim that had come off. He carried buckets of water from a nearby stream. Jean Pierre honed a replacement spoke from a suitable oak limb. When the new spoke was fitted in place, the men used sticks to carry the heated metal rim above the wooden wheel lying on the ground. Carefully, they lowered the hot rim around the wooden wheel. Then they splashed water to shrink the metal tightly around the wooden wheel.

Jean Pierre inserted the metal roller bearings into the hub. Centuries earlier, the Kelts in the Black Forest had invented iron roller bearings for wheels. Jean Pierre and Guy were wrights in that tradition. Wood-shaping and metal-working were all part of the legacy of Keltic Europe.

Satisfied with their work, they fed and watered the horses. In the smoldering fires, they heated soup and tea that they ate with crusty bread. Then the little caravan moved on to Bourges. From the window in cab, Heléne watched her husband following behind the procession and her son in front. At Bourges they clattered along the cobbled streets and through the gates of the royal enclave. There stables, food and beds awaited.

The lecture hall in the Bourges Law College was a small amphitheatre with wooden chairs surrounding an Anglo-Norman dais. The oak panels of the walls and ceiling gave the feeling a well-fabricated cabinet. A glass skylight added to the illumination of the candle-lit setting. The Law College was the centerpiece of the University at Bourges that Louis XI had founded in 1477.

A half-century later his grandniece carried on his work with political savvy. Queen Marguerite was instrumental in bringing Alciato of Milan [1492-1550], a celebrated expert in jurisprudentia to the chair at Bourges. As Duchess of Berry, Queen Marguerite wanted to ensure that this Law College instituted by her forbearer had a significant place in the emergence of French legal humanists.

Previously, at her Law College at Orléans, Marguerite, Duchess of Berry, had enlisted the noted Pierre de l'Estoile.

"A certain rivalry between the humanist jurists in the Duchy of Berry is healthy," Marguerite thought to herself. She recalled that her own father had often gone by the name, Charles d'Orléans du Berry.

Still grasping her riding-whip and wearing her equestrian riding helmet, vest and Gaelic *triubhas,* Queen Marguerite strode into the stately architectural setting of jurisprudence. She paused to view the semi circular amphitheatre. The tiers of seats rose gradually from the central podium. "Louis must have been pleased with this chamber," she thought to herself.

Athletically, Marguerite climbed the risers to the third tier and moved to a seat slightly off-center facing the lectern. Lassie followed judiciously. She sat back and crossed her becoming trouser-covered legs. A person who understood herself, Marguerite relaxed with a nonchalant dignity, and awaited the arrival of Alciato.

The motley mix of students filing into the room was nondescript and unexceptional—some alert, some lackadaisical. The equestrian lady, being the only female present, caused many to cast a quick glance her way. But none dared look her in the eyes.

Below, in the second tier to her left, a wandering scholar sank into his chair. He exhibited an awkward good humor. He glanced around with a faint smile. Probably he had not come with great expectations for the lecture. His face seemed to show a congenial casual curiosity. His backpack and handful of books gave him a certain well-read individuality. She wondered?

On her right, a younger law student sat alone. He appeared to be an outsider. In an adjacent chair, he stowed his knapsack with his worldly goods. He casually scribbled with a stick of sharpened graphite on a note pad. Obviously, he would not be impressed by pretended knowledge. His face suggested a critical, yet open mind. How would he absorb the lecture? Sensing that he was being observed, the younger man cast a furtive glance in the direction of the Queen. Their eyes met for a brief moment.

The professor emerged from an oaken side door in the wood paneled chamber and made his way to the dais.

"He's a bit too short for a Lombard," Rabelais mused to himself out loud so that everyone around could hear.

Marguerite was taken aback but kept her reactions to herself.

"Possibly a Neapolitan? Maybe a Sicilian? But that's unheard of!" Rabelais babbled blatantly to himself allowing all around him to snicker. A student behind him threw an apple core.

The Duchess of Berry continued to wear a composed smile but she was not amused. The serious student on her right read her thoughts in a glance, but he quickly returned his gaze to Alciato taking the rostrum. The professor had obviously not heard the remarks.

"Why am I reacting like this?" Marguerite scolded herself. "In a humanist society, there should be free speech. This law classroom should be a place for give and take!" She re-crossed her eye-catching legs to affirm her newly discovered self-knowledge.

The self-assured Alciato opened his mouth to speak. But when he squeaked in a high pitched falsetto, Rabelais chortled and coughed. Marguerite touched her lips and chin.

Calvin drew a hasty sketch that she glimpsed from the corner of her eye. Marguerite was laughing inside. She had come to the lecture as herself. In her riding habit she was not putting on the airs of a Catherine de Médicis destined for her nephew, Henry.

Queen Marguerite was a humanist by being an honest human being. She was authentic—what you see is what you get. And here she was between a loudmouth satirist and lad caricature sketching her squeaky Italian. In this initial moment of Alciato's lecture, she found herself between two mocking critics—one a buffooning jester, the other a lampooning cartoonist.

With a certain hauteur of superiority, the distinguished Milanese jurist cast a sweeping glance around the room and began his discourse in jurisprudentia…

"*Qui ne sait dissimuler, ne sait regner.*"

"He who knows not how to conceal his intentions, cannot reign."

—Louis XI

«*Les gens font semblant de ne pas aimer les raisins quand les vignes sont trop hauts pour qu'ils puissent atteindre.*»

"People pretend not to like grapes when the vines are too high for them to reach."

—Marguerite of Navarre

...Louis XI fathered modern France...

70 years earlier, Louis XI fathered modern France. Europe was a hodgepodge of duchies, dukedoms, chiefdoms and fiefdoms. Louis envisioned a BIG picture. He reassembled the jigsaw pieces. Louis XI created FRANCE from one end to another.

Instead of wars, Louis XI arranged political marriages. They nicknamed him Louis the Prudent! Louis arranged the marriage of Archduke Maximilian of Austria with Mary, Duchess of Burgundy.

On 24 June 1436 King Louis arranged his own marriage with Queen Margaret of Scotland. She was the daughter of King James I of Scotland.

Louis XI paired up Louise of Savoy with Charles du Orléans, Count of Angoulême. At the time, Louise was only eleven years old! Louise had been born on 9/11 in the Year 1478. Louise gave birth to Marguerite, her firstborn child on the eleventh of May 1492. She had become a mother at fourteen. At sixteen she gave birth to Francis who would become the Renaissance King of France!

Louis XI (1423–1483) was born in Bourges. He was monarch of the House of Valois—the French ruling dynasty 1328—1589.

Louis liked Bourges. Louis built the architectural prototypes for the French Renaissance out of the patterns of Medieval France.

Jacques Cœuer, a merchant of Bourges, built the finest Town House in King Louis' modern France. Constructed on the town ramparts, the architecture of this mansion featured a circular central courtyard with seven turret stairways.

In Bourges in 1477, Louis XI founded his university. Architecturally, the Law College was the centerpiece.

Louis and Margaret elected to establish their royal residence at Tours where the River Cher flowed into the Loire. They chose an island in the stream to site their home. Château de Plessis-lez-Tours became their favorite residence. This early Renaissance château was built in a U-shape in a landscape of gardens in the riverine estuary.

The Loire Valley centered the French Renaissance in a brilliant natural environment. Magnificent châteaux would rise on every imaginable setting. Château de Plessis-lez-Tours foreshadowed the magnificent châteaux of the Loire Valley during the high Renaissance era of Francis I.

Our state is shaken by innumerable storms, and there is only one hope for its future safety; just like a ship in the middle of the sea that the winds grasp, it now breaks up in the briny water. But if the brothers of Helen, shining stars, appear, good hope restores those downcast spirits.

—Alciato, *Book of Emblems*

...a Milanese jurist of some repute...

Alciato [1492-1550] cast a sweeping glance around the room before he began to speak. With certain haughtiness in bearing and attitude, Alciato acquitted himself as a Milanese jurist of some repute. The esteemed Italian in his dress and manner assumed the superiority of things Italian. From his point-of-view, the humanist jurisprudence of Italy was far in advance of anything the French might offer. He was certainly aware that King Francis I had brought many Italian architects and artists to his court including Leonardo da Vinci.

Alciato paused to establish a silent authority in the assembly. Then Alciato began his lecture about the rule of law of the mind of Roman Tacitus.

"In his *The Annals of Imperial Rome*, Tacitus said, 'the more corrupt the state, the more numerous the laws. When the state is MOST corrupt, then the laws are MOST multiplied.' " Another dramatic pause.

Rabelais muttered under his breath, "These pauses are getting to be a habit."

Ignoring this comment, Queen Marguerite looked up at the portrait of Louis XI on the wall. He was wearing his famous hat. She quietly acknowledged to herself that her own riding helmet was similar.

Alciato continued to drag out homologous citations of Tacitus, "The more corrupt the state, the more it legislates."

Calvin listened patiently. At length, he yawned. He caught himself and cast a furtive glance around. Marguerite offered a faint smile. He straightened up and gave Alciato his full attention.

When Alciato paused in his remarks, Calvin raised his hand and commented, "You give a more republican reading of Tacitus than one might have thought appropriate to his politics."

"One would have thought that the son-in-law of General Agricola would have been more imperialistic," chimed in Rabelais, not wanting to miss out.

Alciato coughed. Clearly, he had not expected to be interrupted by his captive audience of law students.

"Certainly Tacitus lived a century after the demise of the Roman Republic," Alciato responded. "The jealous Emperor Domitian did not praise the well-earned achievements of Agricola. And Tacitus was Agricola's son-in-law."

Calvin pushed the point. "Tiberius Gracchus, two centuries earlier, is more deserving of such a republican interpretation of Roman history as you give Tacitus. He saw the small farmer as the backbone of the Roman state."

"You're correct," admitted Alciato. "But Tacitus saw a republican spirit in the Britons. The Romans dominated the Britons for 500 years. And yet the Britons emerged unscathed in 410 to resume their Keltic ways."

Calvin retorted. "Tacitus describes his own Romans in a speech he puts into the mouth of General Calgacus, their enemy: 'The Romans ravage, they slaughter, they seize by false pretenses, and all of this they hail as the construction of empire. And when in their wake nothing remains but a desert, they call that peace'."

...a Milanese jurist of some repute...

Unobserved, Marguerite silently clapped her hands. This classroom reparteé was magnificent.

Rabelais spoke up. "My friend here is quoting a Gallic leader. You Sir are from Milan in Cisalpine Gaul. What say you about Gallic Law? It was much older than Roman Law."

Alciato stared out the window, as though he hadn't heard the question. He shifted from one foot to the other. He evaded giving a direct answer. Instead, he bought time by offering some background on Tacitus' life.

Rabelais caught the eye of Calvin and winked. Marguerite chuckled to herself whilst keeping a straight face towards the professor.

Undaunted, Alciato continued his diversionary tactic. He said, "In the era of the dictator Emperor Domitian, Tacitus was promoted up the steps of the Roman civil service. Tacitus moved up from Aedile, to Quaestor, to Praetor, to Consul. As an Aedile, he was responsible for public works—the grain and water supply. As Quaestor he administrated finances for government and military. As Praetor and then Consul, Tacitus achieved the highest offices in the Roman Empire."

Rabelais had his hand up, but Alciato ignored him.

Alciato rumbled on, "Domitian was very dictatorial. He sent General Agricola to conquer Britain and Germany..."

"But..." interrupted Calvin.

"I'm coming to your point," rejoined Alciato. "The highest officer in Rome puts these words into his mouth of the Gallic enemy: 'The Romans ravage, they slaughter, they seize by false pretenses, and all of this they hail as the construction of empire. And when in their wake nothing remains but a desert, they call that peace'.

"Tacitus would seem to bow to the Gallic general's sense of law and honor," Rabelais spoke up loudly.

"It would seem that this Roman Consul who writes Roman

history is writing a very self-critical judgment," admitted Alciato with a faint smile. "Today I am proud of my Cisalpine Gallic roots!"

Professor Alciato quickly picked up his notes and disappeared. For a long moment the chamber was silent. The architecture of the classroom created a physical and social distance between teacher and students. Perhaps the architect had visualized an imperious pedagogue lecturing to suppliant learners.

It is possible that Alciato saw only Rabelais and Calvin seated close to his lectern. In the theatrical exchange that had taken place, Alciato, Calvin and Rabelais were the players. The scene foreshadowed humanist conversations and disputations to come.

Disentangling his legs, Rabelais extricated himself from his impromptu couch. He gathered his things he moved out. Without looking around, the lanky Calvin stood up, fastened his coat and proceeded to another door. The lives of Rabelais and Calvin might never have intersected again were it not for an invitation…

1423.07.03	Louis XI – Father of France [1461-1483] Valois Dynasty
1436.06.25	Louis XI marries Margaret of Scotland
1461-1522	Anne of France
1477-1514	Anne of Brittany…daughters Claude & Renée
1478.09.11	Louise of Savoy born
1488.02.16	Louise marries Charles Valois
1492.04/11	Marguerite born at Angoulême
1494.09.12	Francis born at Cognac
1494-1553	François Rabelais
1496.01.01	Louise widowed
1509-1564	Jean Calvin
1514.05.18	Francis marries Claude
1515.01.25	Francis I – Renaissance King of France [1515-1547]
1515.09.14	Francis wins back Cisalpine Gaul at Marignano
1515—1529	Louise is Regent of France
1516—1519	Leonardo da Vinci in France
1525	Marguerite marries Henry of Navarre
1528.04	Renée becomes Duchess of Ferrara
1528.11.16	Marguerite has daughter Jeanne d'Albret
1531.09.22	Louise of Savoy dies
1547	Francis I dies
1549.12.21	Marguerite dies
1553.12.13	Jeanne d'Albret has son Henry IV = 1st Bourbon Dynasty

...unnoticed amid the most influential...

Louise of Savoy grew up insignificantly in the shadow of Anne of France—her guardian as it were. To make way for the favored heirs to the throne, Louise was sidestepped. She lived her earliest years inside the great Château Amboise unnoticed amid the most influential people in France. Moving amongst the powerful of French society, her makings were overlooked.

Unobserved, Louise moved south out of the royal Loire Valley to marry Charles de Valois, Comte d'Angoulême. Louise was eleven years old!
Charles had a mistress, Jeanne de Polignac—not eligible for marriage to nobility. Jeanne continued in his household with two brilliant but unrecognized children. The older Mistress Jeanne and the younger Countess Louise lived happily together with Count Charles. So it seemed... Louise gave birth to Marguerite on 11 April 1492 in Angoulême. Louise was then fourteen!

Louise and Charles moved their Angoulême court twenty miles west to the artists' colony of Cognac. They had a superb library of illuminated manuscripts and richly bound books. Living in residence, Jean and Octavien de Saint-Gelais taught all the children. Musicians played for dances and concerts.

Wandering scholars frequented their court. Artists painted their idyllic country landscape.

Francis was born 12 September 1494 at Cognac. This provincial royal era foreshadowed the events that made Francis king and Louise his regent. On 1 January 1496, nineteen-year-old Louise was unexpectedly widowed. They remained at Cognac where Louise raised her children, Marguerite and Francis.

"Paris n'est pas une ville, c'est un monde."

"Paris isn't a city, it's a world."

—King Francis I

...socializing with the female species...

King Francis I loved women. He welcomed lovely ladies at court. Convivially he said, "A court without women is a year without spring and a spring without roses." He was fond of feasting, drinking, and socializing with the female species. He fashioned a brilliant medley of poets, musicians and artists who mingled with the idle nobility. Art, elegance, and chivalry heightened his licentious soirées and lavish galas.

Francis found no incongruity in loving and conceiving a child per year with his Queen Claude while carrying on nocturnal escapades. His father was his role model. In his earliest years at Cognac, Francis watched his father mix it up with Mother Louise and Mistress Jeanne. He viewed it as normal and unremarkable. Like father, like son.

Subconsciously, Francis primary female model was his sister, Marguerite. Two years older, she was his childhood companion. They listened to the same stories. They ate the same food. They played the same games. They rode horses together over the same terrain.

Francis had an early military success. He took back Milan and Cisalpine Gaul for France. This first successful battle went to Francis youthful head. Behaving like Don Quixote, Francis marched further into Italy. And then he met a crushing defeat at Pavia. Charles V imprisoned Francis at Alcazar. Journeying to Spain, Marguerite talked sweetly to Charles to secure her brother's release in exchange for two hostage sons! Once freed, Francis promptly forgot his promises to Charles who was becoming Holy Roman Emperor.

    Francis traveled around France nonstop. He loved showing himself to people who had never seen a king. He became familiar with the geography of his country. During his travels, Francis emptied prisons and curtailed abuses. In his grand manner, he was generous with ordinary people. He encouraged sports and games. The nobility was appalled at their King glad-handing the lowly proletariat.

    Francis waffled between his dreams of a new France and pleasing the medievalists at the Sorbonne. He lacked the prudence and the diplomatic skill of Louis XI.

    Francis was not keeping up with his fermenting French culture. His regent mother and sister, however, were developing a nation of humanists for the future. When Louise died in 1531, Marguerite vigorously carried on the humanist cause.

"The first modern woman," Samuel Putnam calls Marguerite, Queen of Navarre. Sister of Francois I, mother of Jeanne d'Albret, grandmother of Henri IV, author of the "Heptameron" and much poetry, friend of authors, scholars, great men without number, she was the most cultured and learned woman of her period and for long afterward. In his biography of Marguerite, Queen of Navarre, Mr. Putnam refers to her as King François I's "astonishing sister."

—New York Times, 15 December 1935

...the first modern woman...

Marguerite was a beautiful woman. Emperor Charles V was smitten by Marguerite; she was his first love. But Mother Louise saw the diplomatic peril of such a union. Louise attempted to marry Marguerite to the future Henry VIII of England. That didn't happen. Louise quickly married her off to the Duke of Alençon—a noble nobody. In this arrangement, Marguerite had time to support her royal brother and regent mother at court.

Marguerite, it is said by several biographers, became the first modern woman. Her humanist philosophy set the secular and spiritual tone for the modern woman to emerge. In her life, she practiced a humanist approach to solving problems. She was the real mind behind the High French Renaissance.

Marguerite enabled her gregarious, glad-handing, womanizing, malleable brother Francis to succeed. Francis was an impractical dreamer. Marguerite masterminded his better ideas and made them come true. The Collège de France as the first open humanist university. The Law Colleges at Orléans and Bourges. She made it all happen. New chateaux went up along the Loire and Cher. The Louvre was the royal residence.

Her nephew, Henry II thought Aunt Marguerite was the greatest woman who ever lived. Henry womanized Catherine d'Medici and Diane of Poitiers among others. A galloping knight at a tournament tilting at his lady in the royal box, Henry didn't see the long lance coming. Jousted and unhorsed, Henry's time had come.

Queen Marguerite buttonholed two doormen. She quickly grasped the lapels of the nearest.

"That fellow going out the far door," she pointed. "Tell him that the Queen invites him to be her guest at dinner at the Royal Arms at 5."

"…dinner at the Royal Arms at 5," he repeated.

"Off you go," she ordered impatiently.

Then she impounded the second doorman grabbing his sleeve.

"That lanky student shouldering his knapsack," she pointed in the opposite direction.

"Tell him that the Queen invites him to be her guest at dinner at the Royal Arms at 5."

"…dinner at the Royal Arms at 5," the second man repeated.

She pointed and strong-armed the fellow to get moving.

The first doorman caught up with Rabelais.

"Monsieur," he pulled at his sleeve.

"What do you want?" Rabelais squinted in the sunlight.

"The Queen invites you to be her guest at dinner at the Royal Arms at 5."

"What?"

"The Queen invites you to be her guest at dinner at the Royal Arms at 5."

"I heard you, but what Queen?"

"Our Queen. Queen Marguerite of Navarre."

"Not really?" Rabelais said—uneasy with the thought.

"She was seated behind you."

"The equestrian woman with the dog?"

...the first modern woman...

"Yes. She invites you to be her guest at dinner at the Royal Arms. Will you come?"

"How can I say 'NO' to the Queen?"

"...the Royal Arms at 5."

Rabelais straightened up and squared his shoulders. "5 it is."

Calvin lolled idly in a notch in a floral wall by the street. A Picard, he nursed a beer from Picardy and munched a stale end cut of French bread.

The second doorman approached him.

"You were at the Alciato lecture?" the doorman queried.

With sardonic silence, Calvin looked at his questioner.

"The Queen invites you to be her guest at dinner at the Royal Arms at 5."

"The Queen?"

"She was seated near you at the lecture."

"The lady with the collie?"

"Yes. She is Queen Marguerite, Duchess of Berry."

"And she is inviting me?"

"...dinner at the Royal Arms at 5."

"The Royal Arms at 5." the dumbfounded Calvin repeated.

At that moment, Marguerite, still in her riding habit, strode up and extended her hand to Calvin. In deference, he took her hand, doffed his berét and bowed delicately.

"You are coming?" the Queen reaffirmed her invitation.

"Well...yes, of course. It would be an honor. But I'm not dressed..."

The Queen paid no heed. "I'm on my way there now. Why don't you walk with me?"

Leaving his beer and bread on the railing, Calvin stepped to.

"I don't know your name," the Queen opened the conversation.

31

"My name... my name is Jean Cauvin. Lately, it's gotten Latinized to Calvin."

"Monsieur Calvin, you are quite a compelling and aggressive lawyer!"

Calvin was at a loss, but he managed to say, "I'm a bit of a wandering scholar."

"But you study law?"

"Well yes—at Orleans."

"And the Classics?"

"I'm studying Seneca..."

"So you have your law degree?"

"My Masters in Law a year ago. My Doctorate next year."

"With Professeur Pierre de l'Estoile."

"Yes. Do you know him?"

"Yes. I appointed him."

Stupefied, his throat went dry at this rapid-fire information.

"A thousand pardons," he rasped

She was quiet for a moment and then spoke very softly.

"It's part of my job."

"Your job?" Calvin was letting it all slowly sink in...

"Bourges and Orleans are both in the Duchy of Berry."

"Of course," he bowed meekly, "you are the Duchess of Berry...

"For a lawyer, you are quite speechless?" Marguerite laughed amicably at her newest protégé. "You certainly were not tongue-tied with Alciato. You had the lofty Italian in a tizzy."

Calvin was still putting two and two together.

"So you brought both Pierre de l'Estoile and Alciato to their posts..."

Not to be sidetracked, Marguerite pushed on. "Do you talk up to Pierre de l'Estoile like you did with Alciato?"

"My apologies..." deferred Calvin.

"Well...do you?" she repeated.

"Actually…Professor Pierre de l'Estoile encourages disputation and counter arguments."

"Does he?" Queen Marguerite was impressed.

"That's right. A lawyer needs to be on his toes," replied Calvin.

Queen Marguerite stopped in her tracks and turned to look eye to eye at Calvin. She smiled wryly and said, "And you've managed two degrees of law debating fine points with him?"

"Well…I do respect Pierre de l'Estoile very highly. He is a humanist in the best sense."

"So…" Marguerite continued to explore, "you were expecting disputation with Alciato?"

"I had thought…"

"You had thought Alciato would be more on his toes!" she twittered.

"It was a bit disappointing. Alciato didn't really answer my question."

"He equivocated by reciting Tacitus' Roman curriculum vitae…"

"…from Aedile, to Quaestor, to Praetor, to Consul," Calvin continued her sentence. "It's an interesting story, but not the answer to my question."

"Alciato expected acquiescent students, not reparteé," she smiled faintly and glanced at her protégé.

Calvin clutched his béret. His cape flared loosely on his gangly shoulders. He double-stepped to keep up with Marguerite's strides. Her Border collie paced along a few steps ahead.

"We're walking through the university gardens plotted by Louis XI," she directed Calvin's attention to the cloistered landscape with a sweep of her hand.

"King Louis XI had all this in mind," said Calvin, impressed.

"The University with the Law College was his creation. And, of course, these landscaped gardens. Let's sit for a moment by this colonnade facing the quadrangle green."

The law student was quite taken off guard. Never in his wildest thoughts had he expected to sit and converse with the Queen.

"Louis XI was the mastermind who created the modern map of France," she went on. "He was the first of a line of Renaissance Kings. And my brother continues."

Calvin nodded to affirm her words—still clutching his berét.

Then Marguerite shifted herself and looked directly at Calvin.

"I'm looking for an intelligent, aggressive young lawyer to work on a project with my brother. As a humanist, he is looking to develop a new form of government—a humanist form of government for France. From your performance today, I'm thinking that you might be that humanist lawyer we're looking for."

She turned her eyes to face him directly.

Calvin drew back shyly. He was not prepared for such an invitation…

Then without further ado, she got up and continued their trek around the quad.

Arriving at the posh Royal Arms, the maitre d'hotel rushed to attend the Duchess of Berry. He led her to Le Grande Salon of King Louis and Queen Margaret. Polished brass doorknobs and chandeliers glittered in the room. The walls and ceilings of were a cabinetry of oak panels.

Rabelais appeared from the shadows of the velvet drapes that framed the doorway.

Marguerite halted and extended her hand to him. "The other student of law," she said affirmatively. "I am Marguerite, Duchess of Berry," she said. "And you are?"

"My name is François Rabelais." He took her hand with a simple genuflect.

"Monsieur François Rabelais, please meet Monsieur Jean Calvin."

"I recognize you from the lecture," Rabelais acknowledged.

"And I you," said Calvin quietly. Calvin realized that he was somewhat younger than the Queen and Rabelais. By his restraint, he showed them respect. Certainly, he was not going to take over the conversation as he had in the classroom.

"So… Welcome to you both. Let's sit at that table by the doors that open onto the veranda."

The maitre d'hôtel made haste to oblige.

The setting was comfortable in the fading sunlight. The small round table offered an intimacy for thoughtful conversation. The maitre d'hôtel removed a chair so that they sat in a triangle to each other. The evening took on the promise of a warm exchange.

Then the maitre d'hôtel continued, "Our prepared dinner meal tonight is fois gras—stuffed goose. The dessert is an assiette aux fromages—an assorted plate of cheeses."

"That will be very good," said the Duchess. "Is this to your tastes gentlemen?"

Rabelais and Calvin both nodded agreeably. How could they possibly disagree?

"I've a chance to see some of your writing," Calvin deferred to Rabelais without fawning. *"For smiles, not tears, make the better autograph, because to laugh is natural to man."*

Rabelais chuckled appreciatively with a smile, but he said nothing.

Queen Marguerite continued the agreeable small talk, "My experience from often being in the shadows is that laughter just might be the best medicine."

"A good laugh certainly makes you feel better," Rabelais affirmed.

The Duchess smiled at her guests. These two rabble-rousers in the classroom were certainly amicable to each other. It was obvious that the younger man knew of Rabelais and respected his work.

"So…" the Duchess sought to enter the conversation. "You are a writer, Monsieur Rabelais? You are new to me."

"I'm a person in transition," Rabelais gibed back in a self-repudiating manner.

"Your snippets get circulated around the universities—especially Paris," injected Calvin.

"Please inform me!" insisted the Duchess becoming very interested. "Monsieur Calvin, how would you describe his work?"

"Oh…M'lady, I wouldn't begin to…" Calvin evaded.

"I was a priest. Now I'm a satirist," Rabelais interjected bluntly. "Now I satirize priests…"

Calvin came into the conversation. "I was studying to be a priest, but thankfully I discovered the humanists at Orléans."

Rabelais quipped, *"The farce is finished. I go to seek a vast perhaps."*

Calvin gulped, "That's it exactly…"

Not to be outdone, Marguerite said shyly, *"Certainty's a problem because uncertainty is real…"*

To this, Rabelais and Calvin both lifted their wine glasses. But Marguerite continued.

"Once I asked Jacques Lefevre d'Étaples, 'Why are we here? Why is the universe here? Why do we die? Is there any purpose to life?' Jacques eyed me and replied: 'You can say—I don't know. It's honest to admit that you cannot explain the unexplainable.'"

"I'm overwhelmed," Calvin said. "I've studied the scholarship of d'Étaples, but you know him personally."

"I as well," added Rabelais. "He is probably the greatest humanist…"

"Actually," Marguerite admitted, "I'm protecting him right now at my home at Nerac."

They ate and drank in silence. The fois gras was delicious. Soon a young woman arrived with a plate of cheeses with slices of French bread. She brought fresh wine and refilled their glasses.

She offered a faint smile to Calvin who was quite in awe of her attention to him.

"I also write," the Queen continued the conversation. "My model is Boccaccio. His *Decameron*. I write about the foibles of ordinary people in the provincial village where I grew up."

"And where, might I ask, was that?" Rabelais inquired.

"Cognac."

"I grew up a hundred miles north at Poitou. My father was a lawyer. He put me in the local monastery and destined me for the priesthood. Alas…" he sighed.

"I had something of the same fate," said Calvin. "My father was the cathedral bursar so he got me a church scholarship. But the bishop fired him. My tiffed father decided that I should study law."

"Might I ask a favor?" Rabelais addressed the Duchess. "Could you favor us with one of your stories?"

"Yes," interrupted Calvin, "I too would be most interested."

Marguerite eyed her guests. "You honor me. No one has ever made such a request of me. I will try to oblige you."

The young waitress reappeared with more wine.

Rabelais and Calvin raised their glasses to Marguerite and her forthcoming story.

"This story has its setting around my home in Nerac where I live with my husband. This story is a little bit about me. I'm Parlamente. Hircan is my husband."

> Hircan rode back to the chateau from his morning foxhunt. He was early. He slipped in the side door. Entering the Great Hall, he discovered a priest pinning his protesting wife against the tapestries. As Hircan strode across the room, the priest retreated and his wife slipped away behind the curtains."

The day before, Hircan and Parlamente attended mass at the Franciscan Church in Agen. They arrived to find the sermon being preached from the high pulpit by a particular Franciscan priest highly regarded by everyone. In his saintly robes, the women found him to be the handsomest priest in the region. They listened devoutly, their eyes fixed on this venerable friar, their ears hanging on his every word. Beneath the spiritual guise, carnal flames raged in their passions.

Hircan now confronted the haughty priest.
"I've come to your house to ask for alms for the poor," he said unashamedly.
Hircan looked at the priest, "Of course you were…"
The priest held his ground.
"What did you say your name was?"
"Ah… I'm Big Peter…"
"Big Peter," said Hircan. "That fits…"
The priest babbled on. "I'm Big Peter—the hard rock."
"Hard indeed," Hircan sneered. "What are your intentions, Little Peter?"
"Big Peter!" the evasive priest wriggled his codpiece over his tight crotch. Priests are not accustomed to being questioned. But in this case, the King of Navarre was asking.
"Our lives are laid upon female foolishness…"
"Laid?"
"So long as foolish females exist, we shall not die of hunger.'

Hircan moved the chess game of words forward. "So sermons fritter with the foolishness of females?"
At this, Queen Parlamente threw back the curtains. "Priests don't preach to women to become wise. Priests want foolish females to fuck! I get it!"

Hircan pressed the priest against the wall. Hircan baited the sanctimonious priest: "What woman could prevent herself from believing in you? Little Peter."

"I'm Big Peter, damn it. I have a sizable reputation."

Hircan continued "You've been appointed by our Prelates to preach the Gospel and admonish us for our sins!"

The priest duck-walked backwards towards the door.

"Your shtick to propagate the Gospel is very upright," Hircan guffawed. "From the look of that codpiece, I'm sure it is! I'll bet you can loosen your cords most cordially, Cordelier."

"In church, he is good preaching sermons from his lofty pulpit, but when he gets inside our home he is the Antichrist!" screamed Parlamente.

At that moment the Queen's mother, Oisille came into the room. She had been listening at the door. She drew herself up to her full height and glared at the priest: "There is not a single text in Holy Scripture, however beautiful that you would not turn to your own ends. But take care lest, like the spider, you turn wholesome meat into poison. Be assured that it is indeed dangerous to draw on Scriptures to pursue your carnal lusts."

Hircan trenchantly took the Franciscan priest by the upper arm and ushered him to the door.

Rabelais and Calvin were astonished. Men could brandish their banter, but not women! They sat mute.

Rabelais broke the silence. "I'm a Franciscan friar," he grinned.

"I could have told you a ladylike story," she eyed her guests judiciously. "But I haven't got time to waste finding out what kind of humanists you are. We are not dining in Suleiman's harem!"

Calvin weighed in. "I overheard one of Rabelais' stories circulating the university. A giant named Gargantua sends his son, Pantagruel, to check out Paris. Pantagruel towers high above the city. He is really disgusted by what he learns. So he pisses down on the Sorbonne and Notre Dame. Priests die in the flood."

Queen Marguerite showed no shock. Instead, she mischievously smiled at her guests. They were truly humanists appreciating life! Unexpectedly, her *Heptameron* story had opened up the tragicomedy of life. Their threesome staged a theatre of the absurd in their table talk. Without a plan, an existential moment occurred. She invited the two outspoken characters from Alciato's classroom to her table. She had not known their names. But it was really good that she had not known their names. She conversed with them at a human level of understanding.

"But what about your writing?" Calvin questioned Rabelais. "Was Pantagruel your underlying yarn?"

Rabelais pulled a manuscript out of his pouch. He pulled back from the table and stood up:

> My friends, who about to read this book,
> Please rid yourselves of every predilection;
> You'll find no scandal, if you do not look,
> For it contains no evil or infection.
> True, you'll discover, upon close inspection,
> It teaches little, except how to laugh:
> The best of arguments, the rest is chaff,
> Viewing the grief that threatens your brief span;
> For smiles, not tears, make the better autograph,
> Because to laugh is natural to man.

...the first modern woman...

Quite out of character, Queen Marguerite stood up and clapped her hands in applause. Calvin pulled himself together and did the same.

Rabelais pressed his manuscript to his chest and bowed before Marguerite.

"My Gracious Queen," he spoke earnestly in the tragicomedy of the moment, "your story about Parlamente and Hircan made me appreciate the humanity of your soul."

He placed his rumpled manuscript in front of Marguerite on the table.

"As a gesture of my greatest respect, I dedicate *Gargantua and Pantagruel* to you. I place my work in your hands to publish or discard."

Marguerite was astonished and pleased. "Your work will be published," she said.

Then with a flourish of his cape, Rabelais bid adieu.

"Thank you for inviting me to dinner," Calvin fumbled an appreciation to Queen Marguerite.

"It was such a pleasure to have a conversation with you and Rabelais," she responded with a faint smile.

Calvin had not planned his lodging and it was late. He made his way down the dark hotel hallway. He felt so tired. His heavy eyes located a built-in bench in a secluded bay window. He fell asleep with his neck cramped in an uncharitable corner.

He didn't remember when the maid joined him. He roused for a brief moment when he felt the girl cradled next to him. He was so exhausted, but he appreciated her warm closeness. It was years since his beautiful mother had held him close. His drifting mind resonated the humanity of his existence with these new friends...

Homeric Hymn to Askelpius

I begin to sing of Asklepius,
    Son of Apollo,
    And healer of sicknesses.
In the Dotian plain,
    fair Coronis, daughter of King Phlegyas, bare him,
    a great joy to men, a soother of cruel pangs.

—Loeb Homeric Hymns 16

...a wonderful day...thanks to you...

Four years earlier, François Rabelais and Cardinal Jean du Bellay trotted their ponies down the hills of Rome in a carnivalesque spirit.

"When you think about it," said Rabelais, "it's really crazy that we are Augustinians looking for some action in Rome."

"How so?"

"Well…Augustine of Hippo was a real swinger in his youth in North Africa."

"And?"

"He did an about-face and foisted his guilt on us all…"

"You mean no action."

"Yeah…except in Rome—the carnal court of the world."

"Luther visited Rome. Luther was an Augustinian," said the Cardinal. "He didn't like what he saw in Rome."

"Pope Leo dumped Luther," laughed Rabelais. "And now Luther is married!"

"There you have it," said the wizened Cardinal Bellay.

"But Augustine paved the way for this luxuriant golden capital of Christianity," swooned Rabelais. "Now we are privileged to admire Peter's round duomo!"

"His what?"

"His duomo. The hemispheric lid on his cathedral."

"The golden top," said Bellay.

"The expensive golden duomo," Rabelais babbled on, "Augustine's doctrines gave the priest in the Confessional the tools to cash in on penitent Catholics."

"That's being a bit blunt!" admonished the Cardinal.

"Have you ever watched the Augustinian friars of the Sorbonne in action?" asked Rabelais. "They don't leave a stone unturned. Pay up or burn!"

"In Rome the Pope certainly lives lavishly," admitted Cardinal Bellay. "He's spent a fortune on his extravagant wardrobe. He lays on sumptuous banquets. He sets his table with silver and gold plates. The elite of the Holy Roman Empire dine gluttonously with courtesans."

"Hey! Look who's here!" exclaimed Rabelais. "It's Erasmus. He's holding forth on a poet's dais underneath that ancient column."

"You're right. Erasmus likes to carry on with Cardinals."

In the street opposite the old Roman forum, unrestrained Cardinals romped openly with sensuously dressed cortigiano. Rabelais couldn't resist ogling their suggestive movements.

"You'd better watch out!" shouted Bellay. "You don't have a red hat. The Polizia di Stato Ispettorato di Pubblica Sicurezza Vaticano will whisk you away."

"I need a few Guardian Angels if they are all like this!" goggled Rabelais. "Let me have your red hat!"

Sensuously dressed courtesans grasped their arms. Bellay and Rabelais were awash in a sea of crimson cardinals and their consorts. The Holy City of Christianity energized the carnal desires of the Holy Father and his Holy Cardinals. The red tops caroused freely in the Earthy City of Augustine.

"Hello Jean du Bellay!" Erasmus spotted his friend from

...a wonderful day...thanks to you...

his impromptu pulpit. "Where's your red bonnet? Did your red ribbons come loose?"

"Hello Desiderius Erasmus!" the Diplomat turned Cardinal shouted back. "Have you lost your wits?"

Rabelais returned his red hat and waved at Erasmus.

Erasmus straightened his back and abruptly jerked out a salute with his hand to his forehead.

"Here's to the praise of folly," Rabelais mocked Erasmus' book to Martin Luther—*In Praise of Folly.*

Jean du Bellay couldn't resist the burlesque moment. "Did you hear that Luther got married?" he asked Erasmus.

Erasmus climbed down and came over to his friends.

"Maybe Luther's trip to the Holy City of Carnality loosened him up a bit?" Erasmus commented. "Are you enjoying yourself?"

"What does it look like?" laughed Bellay.

"So what are you fellows in Rome about?" Erasmus asked.

"Well...along with everything else, we wanted to chat with Leo."

"Pope Leo is indisposed right this minute," Erasmus chuckled. "His German fräulein has come to town."

"Maybe she knows Luther's fräulein?" Rabelais joked.

"Cardinal Jean du Bellay, Desiderius Erasmus, and François Rabelais! To what do I owe this pleasure?" the Pope Leo inquired. "What are you in Rome about?"

"I'm here seeking a signature," Rabelais acknowledged.

"A wandering scholar seeking my signature," the Pope chuckled. "And what undertaking are you up to?"

"To continue my medical studies, I wish to be excused of my monastic duties with the Franciscans."

"Done," pronounced the Pope. "Let's have a glass of wine."

Rabelais took a boat from Ostia, the port of Rome. He sailed to the ancient port of Empuries in Catalonia. A rival of Marseilles in ancient times, Empuries circled a protected bay by the sea. The Phoenicians originally developed this natural harbor. They marketed their goods in this emporium—hence the name 'Empuries'.

The Phoenicians constructed a stepped-wharf that allowed sailors easy access to boats whatever the stage of the tides. These Bedouin of the Sea quickly loaded and unloaded their cargoes. These Phoenician sea merchants hoisted on their flat-bottomed ships onto their sides for repair. They scraped off barnacles and applied tar.

Subsequently, in the history of Empuries, the Greeks arrived. They built a hospital. They erected a statue of Aesklepius—their god of medicine. Enshrined on the wall of their seaside clinic was a relief of the rod of Asklepius, a snake-entwined staff. His symbol of medicine has continued.

Aceso, Iaso, Hygieia, Panacea, and Aegle were Asklepius' daughters. Goddess Aceso supervised the healing process. Goddess Iaso enabled recuperation. Goddess Hygieia promoted personal hygiene to preserve health. Goddess Aegle maintained the beauty of the human body. Goddess Panacea was the Druidess cure-all who also invented pancakes.

When the Romans arrived, they maintained the port of Empuries and expanded the town up the hill. Streets were squared off in a Roman gridiron patter. Renovating the hospital, the Romans Latinized Asklepius to Aesculapius.

Earlier in his life, Rabelais had studied medicine. He interned in Lyon at the Hôtel-Dieu hospital. After that, he sought the Pope's permission to continue in medicine.

Rabelais sat down on the beach and contemplated the statue of Asklepius.

"Oh worthy Asklepius! Where are you? I can't see you."

"Here I am," a little boy said pouring sand on Rabelais' bare feet.

"What do you know about that?" Rabelais was jolted out of his reverie.

"Are you Asklepius?" he asked.

"No. I'm Jason."

"Jason are you! Have you found your sheep?"

"What sheep?"

"In the story, Jason was looking for the Golden Fleece of a sheep."

"I didn't know that. But we have two sheep and five lambs."

"Well, I declare. Two sheep and five lambs."

"Want to go for a swim?"

"I was thinking about that."

"You were. So let's swim. Do you skinny dip?"

"You mean naked?"

"Yeah. I like to swim naked."

"Okay…" Rabelais looked around at the empty beach. Then he took off his clothes and followed the boy down the beach. They splashed each other and beat the waves of the Mediterranean.

"Let's float," the boy said.

"Okay…on our backs."

They lay back breathing deeply into their lungs. The two floated with their toes sticking up and eyes closed to the blazing sun. It was marvelous.

"Two fishes floating on the waves," a voice came out of the blue.

"Mommy…you found me," Jason said.

Rabelais threshed in the water to get himself upright and see what was going on.

"Hello…" the soft voice of Mommy addressed him.
"Oh Hi, I'm François."
"I'm Iolantha."
"You have Greek names—Jason and Iolantha."
"Yes. Being close to this Greek port I suppose, but we are Iberian."
"You mean the original Iberian people?"
"That's right," Iolantha said rising up out of the water and exposing her beautiful breasts.

Rabelais suddenly became self-conscious—a rarity with him. Here he was in his birthday suit with Jason splashing in the Mediterranean… And Mommy shows up…

Jason was out of the water clambering over the ruin of the ancient hospital. The statue of Asklepius attracted him and he was climbing up to his bronze shoulders. And then he fell…

"My shoulder, my shoulder," Jason screamed.

Rabelais was out of the water racing to the boy immediately.

"His shoulder is out of joint," he said to Iolantha.

"Can you fix it?"

"I can," he said. "I'm a physician. You hold Jason's body and I will fix his shoulder."

"Will it hurt?" Jason asked still screaming in pain.

"It will be all better in a moment."

With a quick twist Rabelais put the boy's shoulder back in place. Then he held the boy—gently massaging his shoulder, neck and arm.

He watched Iolantha walk down the beach to get their clothes. The sensual movements of her natural beauty contrasted with the carnivalesque carnality of Rome. Saint Augustine's doctrines of celibacy, virginity and second-rate motherhood had cost Christian civilization a heavy price.

"How are you feeling?" Rabelais asked Jason.

"A lot better," Jason smiled. "You are a good doctor."

Rabelais continued to gently rub his back and shoulder.
"On the boat coming here, I caught some fish."
"How did you do that?" asked Jason
"A string with a worm on a hook."
"Does that work?"
"Well…there are three fish."
Jason was amazed.
"I was going to make a fire."
"To cook the fish?" Jason queried.
"One for Mommy. One for Jason. One for me."
"We could fry them at our home. We're not far."
"Probably Jason needs to get home," Rabelais said.
"If I carry your backpack and the fish…."
"That leaves me to carry Jason…"
He cradled the boy in his arms.

"Welcome to the Land of the Indigets," Iolantha said.
"Indigets?"
"Indigets are the Iberian tribe that live in this region."
"We were here first," chimed in Jason.
"Before the Phoenicians, Greeks, or Romans," said Iolantha.
"That would be the time of the Gaul's," Rabelais added.
"And Gaul's mixed with Iberians to be Celt-Iberians."
"And some of the Gaul's and some of the Celt-Iberians sailed north to Ireland. In Ireland they were called Gaels."
"Wow!" said Jason. "That's a lot."

The ruins of an ancient casement wall encircled the little hamlet. Inside stone houses with flat roofs clustered around small gardens. The small streets spoked into a central meeting place. Stalls for a weekly market were there. And a central well provided water.
"Here is our little abode," Iolantha welcomed Rabelais. An arbor of overhanging grape vines sheltered the path to the door.

Pottery was strewn around the little patio everywhere—on ledges, on shelves, and on the floor in corners.

"I'm a potter. An Indiget potter like my mother before me." She pointed to a beehive shaped kiln and a potter's wheel.

"I like that pot with the gargoyle face," said Rabelais.

"You can't have it," said Jason. "My mother made it for me!"

"Okay."

"I'll make a similar pot for you," Iolantha intercepted the problem.

"May I sleep on the roof?" Rabelais asked—putting down his backpack.

"We all can sleep up there."

"I'll sleep next to Jason and massage his shoulder while he goes to sleep."

"Do you tell stories?" Jason asked.

"For sure."

The fish tasted good with some white wine from their homegrown grapes.

Rabelais carried Jason up to their bed on the roof. They lay down together and Rabelais massaged Jason's shoulder.

"Do you see that bright star over there?" Rabelais asked Jason. "That's Asklepius. You were climbing on his statue when you fell."

"Really?" Jason was impressed. Then he said, "What about a good story?"

"How about the story of Jason and The Golden Fleece?"

"A story about me?"

"A boy named Jason like you."

"Please tell me that story!"

>Once upon a time, the God Hermes sent a boy and a girl far away riding on a ram with wings and

...a wonderful day...thanks to you...

fleece of pure gold. They flew over mountains and plains and valleys.

The ram bore them safely to the sacred grove of the God Ares. There they hung up the beautiful Golden Fleece. A dragon was assigned to keep it safe.

A prince named Jason was supposed to become a King of Greece. But his uncle wouldn't let him be king unless he brought him the Golden Fleece. So Jason and his Argonauts sailed a ship named Argo to search for the Golden Fleece. For many days they journeyed on. They came to a narrow place. They were told, "Watch the flight of a dove as it goes between the rocks." They watched the dove and followed it through.

Jason and his Argonauts finally reached the country of the Golden Fleece. Jason asked the cunning king for the Golden Fleece. "No!" the king said. "…unless you can do two things." The First was hitch up two mighty bulls that breathed fire and plow a field that had never been tilled. The Second was pass between warriors while sowing seed in a furrow.

The cunning king's daughter, Medea fell in love with Jason and wanted to help him.

Medea gave Jason magic to enable the bulls to plow the field. Medea told Jason how to trick the warriors to fight each other so that he could pass by.

Then, Medea put the dragon to sleep that guarded the Golden Fleece. Jason grabbed the fleece. The Argonauts were already on the good ship Argo. Then both Jason and Medea climbed aboard and they sailed away with the Golden Fleece.

When they got back home, Jason's uncle still wouldn't let him be king. But Jason and Medea wanted to be King and Queen. As usual, Medea found a way. She tricked his evil uncle and got the kingdom. And then Jason and Medea became King and Queen to live happily ever after…. Well, most of the time.

Jason was fast asleep.

Iolantha was tidying up the kitchen when Rabelais came back down from the roof.

"In spite of the fall, Jason really had a wonderful day… thanks to you," she said. "You are probably wondering about my husband."

"It did cross my mind."

"We live in a corridor between Spain and France where armies pass. Emperor Charles V returned from waging war in Italy. Charles had the King of France as his prisoner."

"Francis I …" said Rabelais astonished.

Iolantha put her hands over her ears. "I can hear the clopping boots marching in step. Then the halt… Then the silence… Then that horrid shout, '*Carpe diem.*' And seize they did. Hungry soldiers set free to seize, plunder, pillage, rape, and loot our little village. We were Soldiers' Pay."

"The Spoils of War," Rabelais parabled with chagrin.

"Jason and I are alive because my husband defended our home. A soldier bayonetted my husband for sport."

"Then on to the next village…march, march, march," Rabelais lip-synched with deep irony in his voice.

"Emperor Charles trashes his aboriginals. We abide in his corridor of war."

From above, Jason cried out.

Rabelais dashed up the tiny stairway and sank to the mat. Lying down beside Jason, he tenderly massaged the boy's shoulder. They both fell asleep.

Iolantha blew out the candle and sat with her thoughts. Then she slowly went to the rooftop and snuggled down beside the boy and the man.

"Est-ce la foi de ne rien comprendre et de soumettre implicitement vos convictions à l'Église?"

"Is it faith to understand nothing, and merely submit your convictions implicitly to the Church?"

—Jean Cauvin

...The Samaritan helps... No strings attached...

Four years earlier in 1528 with a *Licensie des Arts*, Jean Cauvin graduated and was packing up. A new student was taking his room at the College Montaigu in Paris.

"This has been a good room for study," he said. "It's a corner room at the end of the hall. They don't bother you so much."

"Who bothers?" asked Ignatius Loyola.

"It's not the other students. It's the prowlers late at night…"

"Prowlers?"

"The cordeliers, you know… the friars, the monks, the priests… they need a little nookie at night," Cauvin informed the new student.

"Nookie?" queried Ignatius.

"Forced sex… My father was important at Noyon Cathedral. So they were afraid to pick on me. It's the poor boys that have a problem. Like next door. His asshole is sore all the time. I think he's picked up a disease."

"My grandfather is the mayor of Pamplona."

"That should keep the wolves at bay."

"I hope so."

"I knew a locksmith in Noyon. He gave me a bolt for the door."

"A bolt?"

"It's a sliding iron pin. I drilled a hole in the doorjamb and another in this heavy door. This molding covers it up. Just move this molding aside. Put a stick in this hole in the bolt and slide it into the jamb."

"Let me try that."

"There is another feature to this room," said Cauvin.

"What's that?" asked Ignatius.

"Because it's a corner room, it has a window facing the square like the other rooms along the hall. But on the alley, this room has another window that will unlock and open."

"Do they know about this?"

"No. It's a double hung window. They nailed it. But I took out the nails. This is how I'm leaving now."

"It's been a pleasure to meet you," said Ignatius Loyola

"I'd like to stow a small pouch here," Jean Cauvin said. "I'll pick it up later when I come back to Paris."

"Okay."

"I have two copies of *Imitating Jesus* by the Sisters of The Common Life of 1374. I'll give you one if you like?" offered Cauvin.

"That's generous. Thanks much," said Ignatius. It became his favorite book.

When Jean Cauvin was seven, his mother tutored Marguerite del La Roque at the Chateau Roberval a few miles down the River Oise from Noyon. Jeanne Le Franc took her son along. She was a beautiful woman who bequeathed her imposing facial features to her son. In the timber-framed Library, she taught Marguerite and Jean the stories of their history. Afterwards, the Duchess would join her for tea while the children ran about the vast grounds of the Chateau.

On one such day, 13 August 1516, the young King Francis I

...The Samaritan helps... No strings attached...

brought the future Emperor Charles V into the Chateau Library to sign the Treaty of Noyon. At the Battle of Marignano, Francis had retaken the Duchy of Milan. The Duke of Roberval was also present to witness the Treaty between the two Kings. Roberval had soldiered with Francis on this Italian campaign. As friends, they often hunted on the Roberval lands. Later, Francis would send Roberval to be the first Lieutenant General of New France.

The world was his oyster when King Francis I recaptured Milan. The Pope embraced him with accolades. He was positioned to be Holy Roman Emperor. Francis and Charles signed the Treaty of Noyon.

And then at the Battle of Pavia, Charles V knocked Francis off his pedestal. The chess game shifted. Like schoolboys fighting, Charles imprisoned Francis in Spain.

On horseback, Marguerite rode all the way to Spain to rescue her incarcerated brother. Actually, there was more to it. She was Charles' first love. She could turn Charles' head. She secured Francis release and he signed on the dotted line—a signature of no lasting value.

Jeanne Le Franc had married Gerard Cauvin, a boatman on the River Oise. She was the daughter of a Noyon merchant. Her influence enabled Gerard to rise from boatman to city clerk to Procurator of the Noyon Cathedral. Gerard kept the key to the big money chest.

At Noyon in 629, Dagobert had become King of the Franks. Dagobert asked Saint Éloi to found an abbey that later became Noyon Cathedral.

As Procurator, Gerard Cauvin arranged for his sons Charles and Jean to receive scholarship revenues from the first altar on the right—*la Gésine Virgini puerperae*. Jean dedicated his first publication to Saint Éloi—*A Commentary on Seneca*.

While he was still in the good graces of the pretentious Bishop,

Gerard Cauvin destined Jean for the priesthood by sending him to Paris—first to the College March and then College Montaigu.

But then, Gerard Cauvin and his oldest son Charles fell out with the imperious Bishop. Indignantly, Gerard changed Jean's vocation to Law.

Tap,tap…tap,tap…tap,tap…TAP.

"Fa-ther…the-son…ho-ly…GHOST," Ignatius chanted as he opened the alley window to Cauvin's tapping.

"I came back for my pouch." Cauvin brushed himself off.

"I have some sad news," Ignatius condoled. "Word came that your father has died…"

Cauvin paused and looked off into space….

Then Ignatius picked up the slack, "I've been reading *Imitating Jesus.*"

"And…"

"It's the next best thing to the Bible itself!"

"It's a better way than imposing an ideology on someone."

"In his steps," mused Ignatius. "What would Jesus do?"

"Jesus gave people hope…not some sacramental absolution," Calvin commented.

"No hocus pocus for profit," Ignatius followed up.

"The Samaritan helps the beaten man… No strings attached."

"A Fabulous Pearl is about finding life here and now."

"You must have read the whole book!"

"Three times…"

"In the great schemata of God, we are really quite small, nominal creatures. Jesus would have us glorify God and enjoy this precious gift of life we've been given."

"Amen to that."

"I've been with humanists at the Law College in Orléans. In

...The Samaritan helps... No strings attached...

the Classics they find our human life central. We are living in a rebirth of humanity in God's wonderful world."

"Right," said Ignatius. "Imitating Jesus... Keep it simple. Our pedantic dons make doctrines inexplicable: 'How many angels can dance on the head of a pin?' So what!"

"I'm glad I changed to Law. My father freed me from wearing the cloth."

To Jean Cauvin, the humanist Law College at Orléans offered a liberating light at the end of the tunnel. The Classics—Seneca, Ovid, Herodotus, Cicero, and Jesus—presented an alternative that spoke of life. The importance of living life itself thundered in his soul. Cauvin's first publication was a *Commentary on Seneca* dedicated to Saint Éloi.

In 1528 Cauvin began to study secular humanist Law at Orléans under the distinguished Pierre de l'Estoile—an interpreter of Roman Law.

There were about 4000 students at the Law College in Orléans divided into ten French provincial groups. Being from Noyon, a town in Picardy, Cauvin was elected Procurator of the Picardy caucus.

Continuing to read the Classics, Jean Cauvin adopted the name Calvin—harking back to Gnaeus Domitius Calvinus, a Roman senator and loyal partisan of Julius Caesar.

In 1532 Jean Calvin received *Bachelor of Law* at Orléans. A year later, he attained his *Doctorate in Law*.

Throughout his life—even in exile, Calvin never took the cloth but always wore the tabs of a humanist French Renaissance lawyer.

"True, Francis I the French King might have broken with Rome and, like Henry VIII, become the titular as well as the practical Head of the Church. There was an old and strong tradition of Gallicanism in the French…Here lies the significance…If I am inclined to stress <u>organization</u> over against doctrine or anything else, the reason is my profound conviction of its vital importance. Much of English history, Scottish history, and Dutch history might be written round the <u>organization</u> during the Age of Calvin… with his legal training and the clarity and rigour of the French genius…the Gallic qualities of his mind… It is not the theology, it is the <u>organization</u>…better known to most of us by the name Presbyterian…laity elders joined with educated ministers in parity to govern… Democracy was the very essence…among both officers and rank and file… Calvin was the first modern democrat."

—J E Neale, master of 16th Century history

...Was it all a dream?...

The slow staccato of the bell in the university tower clamored eight times and awakened Calvin from deep sleep. He found himself cramped on a wide bench between two cupboards in the hotel anteroom. A sleeping girl was nestled in his arms. Then he began to remember the night before as if it were a dream—

"The Queen invites you to dinner..." Fois gras, wine and cheese. A pretty maid leaned in front of him pouring wine and more wine. The *Heptameron* story the Queen told to get a reaction. The story aroused a strong aversion in him. And yet it forced him to reckon with his own humanity.

"How could..." he rubbed his head, "how could an inept bumpkin like myself—messing about in law and classics...how could I wind up casually table talking with the Queen of Navarre and François Rabelais?"

"Thank you for inviting me to dinner," he had fumbled appreciation to Queen Marguerite.
"It was such a pleasure to have a conversation with you and Rabelais," she responded with an illusory smile.

And then the evening was over, or so he thought.

Was it all a dream? Was it all something he had made up after that classroom fracas? He had not planned his lodging and it was late. He made his way down the dark hotel hallway. He felt so tired. His heavy eyes located a built-in bench in a secluded bay window. He fell asleep with his neck cramped in an uncharitable corner.

He didn't remember when the maid joined him. He roused for a brief moment when felt the girl cradled next to him. He was so exhausted. But he appreciated her warm closeness. It was years since his beautiful mother had held him close. His drifting mind resonated the humanity of his existence with these new friends. And then the dream was over...

The bell clamored out eight o'clock in the university quadrangle. The girl moved in his arms. "Are you awake?" she asked. "This has been so nice."

Now he came to his senses. "I'm as ill-behaved as the Queen's tale," he undertoned to his libido.

But he didn't move. He was gentle. She brushed her hair back and gave him a peck on his lips. He froze.

Nimbly, she moved off the narrow bench and stood up watching him. He swiveled his legs onto the floor and stretched his arms.

"Give me a second Jean," she said. A moment later she came back and offered him an apple with a crust of bread and cheese.

"How do you know my name?" he flushed.

"I was serving the Duchess table. How could I not know?" she flung back.

"But I don't know yours..."

"Didn't you hear the Duchess address me?"

He was at a loss, a great loss at this untimely moment.

"I'm afraid that I didn't hear it," he fessed up despondently.

She laid her hand on his shoulder catching his dispirited soul.

"My name is Brigitte!" she said brightly.

...Was it all a dream?...

Shyly and in awe, he quickly kissed her on both cheeks French style. Then he grabbed his knapsack and bolted for the door. She laughed at the antics of his departure.

On the road again, Calvin set out for Orléans on a path beside L'Yévre River. He had not gone far when a moving procession overtook him. It was Queen Marguerite.

Luc on the lead horse trotted past Calvin. Then came the four-horse hitch pulling the carriage. Jean-Pierre followed along behind. Chattering away, François Rabelais was seated up on top with Guy the driver.

Calvin couldn't help being impressed when the whole entourage clattered to a last hoof clop and then silence. Jean-Pierre dismounted to open the carriage door and Queen Marguerite popped her head out.

"I need you," she said peremptorily to Calvin—putting an end to any refusal.

The young lawyer nodded and looked into her eyes questioningly.

"My brother and I need you."

"You mean the King? How does he know anything about me?"

"In these matter, I speak and act for my brother."

Calvin was astonished.

"Yesterday your performance commanded the classroom discourse. Alciato played second fiddle. Rabelais the cello," Marguerite enchanted a recital of what had happened.

"Was it chamber music or cacophony?" Calvin tried to laugh and downplay the compliment.

"A little of both. That was why it was so superb," she bewitched him graciously.

Rabelais guffawed when he heard her equate him with a cello. He stood up tall and mimicked a cellist on the roof. "Dah-da da-da DÁH dáh…"

Calvin shaded his eyes from the sun with his hand and spoke, "You are too kind, M'lady… Is that how I should call you?"

"We need names that enable us to communicate easily. I like 'Marg,' but I suppose that might be too familiar."

"How about Queen Marg?" Rabelais shouted down.

Marguerite expressed pleasure—inclining to the name.

"This Rabelais is as forward as Calvin is timorous," she evaluated to herself.

Calvin hesitated and then said, "…but in proper company, 'Queen Marguerite?'"

She smiled, "I think I know enough about you to realize that you are the person who can help us."

Marking time Calvin still stood flat-footed in the middle of the road. He was clearly caught off guard. Marguerite was amused at his meekness. This fellow had self-confidence in disputation, but a shy-faced social behavior.

"Please get in," she enjoined him. "This is Heléna my handmaid."

He seated himself beside Heléna. Lassie, the Border collie, nuzzled between his knees and he rubbed her head which did not go unnoticed.

The Queen tapped the ceiling. Luc moved out in front. The horses tightened in their harness and the carriage clattered forward. Amenably, Jean-Pierre on his roan stallion brought up the *rere guarde*.

"My brother and I want to plan a humanist government for France," she stated voluntarily without small talk.

"That's a lot," Calvin managed to say—trying to take it all in.

"We're not going far," she said after a short silence. "It's a bastide."

"A bastide?"

"Yes. A fortified community of peasants."

"They live in a fort?"

"Yes. They live inside, but their farms and gardens and pastures surround the bastide outside."

"Who is attacking them?"

"The seigneurs, the bishops, the dukes—feudal lords of ancien régimes. One of the sports of the nobility is to vandalize bastides."

"But why?"

"They are the elite 1%. They take advantage. They levy taxes based on medieval claims. Then, they have the gall to suggest "austerity measures." Lacking in sensitivity, the elites shamelessly misquote Jesus—'The poor you will always have as a basket of deplorables…'"

"And so it goes…" shrugged Calvin.

"Nonsense," barked Marguerite. "It doesn't have to be that way."

Calvin rubbed Lassie's neck and head. Then he ventured into vulnerable territory where he was defenseless. But it was now or never. "Not to be impertinent or disrespectful, but it seems to me that you and your brother are part of that elite nobility…"

She caught his eye and did not take offense. "You are absolutely right. But the fact that you are graduating from Orléans Law College means that you also are part of the elite." She had him and he nodded.

"You're good!" Marguerite spellbound his submission in a way that didn't offend.

Then her words marched on. "Francis and I want to change all this. France will become a new-mown field. We haven't much time."

"Not much time? How so?" he sought information realizing that for Marguerite this was not a matter for speculation. It was obvious she was thinking of the larger picture. But, to illustrate what she meant, she deferred to a specific incident in the front of her mind.

"My nephew is flirting with a Médicis girl from Italy."
"Is this bad?"
"Henry will succeed his father as king…"
"Yesterday, her Médicis relative was part of a hunting party organized by the Bishop. They galloped over the very bastide gardens we are about to visit."
"How do you mean?" Calvin shook his head. "They…?"
"They intentionally trampled the fields and vegetable gardens. It is their right—so they say."
"How do the peasants deal with it?" Calvin's outrage was growing. His faced flushed with memories of dealing with harsh and oppressive overlords in the Sorbonne bureaucracy.
"Today, the bastide folk are out there in the gardens fixing things. Hoeing. Splinting Replanting. Mulching. Watering."
Calvin was silently thoughtful. This Duchess knew all about gardening. What's more it was obvious that she cared deeply about the plight of ordinary people.

Yesterday he was in a classroom disputation about the theory of law. Today, there was a real moral question staring him in the face. How do you formulate law into practice? How do you organize and apply law in an actual working society.

The bastide was Villeneuve-sur-Cher. A moat around the bastide connected to the River Cher. A dusty road found its way to a bridge over the moat. Their carriage squeaked through a stone arched gate half buried in the built-up berm of earth surrounding the bastide. This protective earthen wall formed the backside of fortified houses facing in. A portcullis mounted in vertical grooves could quickly close the gate.

Once inside, they halted in the central market. Stalls

displayed fruit, vegetables, cloth, pottery and tools. With Queen Marguerite, Heléne and Rabelais, Calvin moved through the sellers and buyers in the crowded stalls. It was market day.

A grape-vined arboretum sheltered a small school where a teacher was listening to students. The children were reciting reading, writing and arithmetic. Their learning was directly applied to the market. Calvin's parochial school in Paris did not equip him for life experience. Priests looked askance and disapproved of the very idea of a mixed classroom. Here boys and girls learned together under the climbing vines of the latticed shelter. He recalled that he had never interacted with girls in a classroom in his entire primary and secondary schooling. His exposure to Queen Marguerite in their table talk and his brief encounter with Brigitte brought him to a new level of human experience and understanding. How better to size up a life partner than to learn together and converse with girls and women in the process of life?

The arboretum also served as a community gathering-place for politics or storytelling, singing and dancing. A small café served coffee to villagers. A mix of young and old were playing a game of Pétanque where steel boules are tossed towards a jack. Jean-Pierre, Heléne went for coffee. Guy and Luc watered the horses and brushed them down; then they sauntered off to join a game of Pétanque.

"This is an impressive place," Calvin expressed an immediate reaction. "The community is in control. Women and men, girls and boys are all involved together."

"I surmise that you have not had much exposure to the opposite sex?" Marguerite queried Calvin with a glint in her eye.

"Actually, I have not. But I think I'm on a learning curve that is spiraliing upward at lightning speed," Calvin acknowledged.

"I was a late bloomer myself," chortled Rabelais. "I love to talk to women! They have a perspective that's not passive."

Marguerite guided them to a raised platform where they could survey the entire social scene. "This is a model for the government and society of our new France," asserted Marguerite with enthusiasm.

"I admire your optimism," laughed Rabelais with gusto. "If anyone can make the future better, it's you, Queen Marg!"

She eyed Rabelais with a faint suspicion that soon evaporated from her face. The she said, "You know, no one has every called me 'Queen Marg' until today. And that's the second time you've said it."

"A thousand pardons I beg of you," Rabelais responded in panic. "I meant no offense. I really apologize for becoming so familiar."

"No!" she rebutted. "I asked for it this morning in my banter. And, I like it! I just have to become accustomed to it. It is very human. And that's what we are striving for—humanity."

"Queen Marg," Calvin addressed her, "you have bridged the distance. I thank you."

"Thank you…Jean," she pressed his hand.

Then she removed her glove and offered Rabelais her hand. With deep emotion, the satirist kissed her hand. There was no mockery in his feelings or actions.

Marguerite moved easily amongst people. Her father, Charles d'Angoulême introduced a potentially explosive state of affairs in their country court at Cognac. Jeanne de Polignac was his older presiding mistress and mother of two of his children. Louise of Savoy was his legal "heiring" bride. Louise was young when they married. Marguerite was born. Then Francis appeared. Marguerite and Francis lived their earliest years with a mother and a mistress who got along satisfactorily. Louise and Jeanne accepted each other and worked things out.

Shortly after, Charles died. His mistress and his wife continued to live together peaceably under one roof. The hodgepodge of this

...Was it all a dream?...

extended family was normal for Marguerite and Francis growing up. Marguerite's great classic, *The Heptameron* reflects this family pandemonium at Cognac.

Now...Francis and Marguerite wanted the inclusive, extended family of France to become normal. The incongruities of humanity—high born and low born—would be gradually normalized, accepted and tolerated in the newer, more democratic society they envisioned.

Surprisingly, King Francis rode up on a white stallion accompanied by a handful of his Scots guards.

"So...what's for lunch?" Francis abruptly asked the café waitress.

"Boeuf bourguignon—braised beef cubes simmered in a seasoned red wine sauce with mushrooms, carrots, and onions."

"A grass-fed calf butchered day-before-yesterday!" the chef chimed in.

"Excellent!" said Francis.

"And a carafe of red wine from your vineyards," added Marguerite.

"Bon Appétit!" saluted Rabelais.

Calvin was overwhelmed. He was sitting with the King, his sister and Rabelais. And this bastide community environment was so totally human.... so like a big family....

"In our childhood, Marguerite and I rode our horses to many bastides in Navarre," Francis said.

"And in Cathar country in the south, bastides are everywhere—especially on mountain tops." added Marguerite.

"The Cathars set the precedent for spreading bastides across France," Francis further noted.

Rabelais laughed with deep irony, "From their bastide summits, they could see the Pope's troops coming from all directions."

"For a man who parties with the Pope, you certainly don't show much respect!" Marguerite mocked.

Rabelais was undeterred. "I practiced medicine at Narbonne near Carcassonne—a magnificent Cathar castle complex. I visited Foix, Montesegur, Mirepoix, and La Bastide-de-Sérou. Every summit bastide is a breathtaking trek."

"It sounds like you did a lot of trekking!" commented Francis who appreciated the tragicomedy of this personable Rabelais.

"I did. The Cathars set the standard for a more humane and compassionate France. The Cathars love to dance and sing, eat and drink. I was always welcome in a Cathar bastide."

"The Cathars were fed up with medieval monks," Calvin showed his irks. "The friars promoted illiteracy, peddled salvation for profit, and pushed the penitential sacraments."

Rabelais picked up on the irony of the Church. "So…the Cathars taught their kids to read." He looked around with a feigned innocence to see if his sarcasm was appreciated.

"Reading…" Marguerite joined him sardonically, "is a deadly sin!"

"Reading Jesus' Parables," Rabelais had dropped his voice an octave, "adds up to heresy!"

King Francis became deadly serious. "Heresy enough to burn 20,000 children, women and men at Albi."

"And 300 Jews," Calvin finished mordantly. They were all familiar with tragedy of the Cathars.

The Teacher at Villeneuve-sur-Cher sat down at their table. "Welcome to Villeneuve-sur-Cher," he said. A young woman joined him. "My name is Iker. This is my wife Xita."

"Xita sounds Catalonian," said King Francis with a smile.

"It is," she responded, "I am a Catalonian gypsy."

"And I'm Spanish from Alcazar."

…Was it all a dream?…

"I was once in prison in Alcazar," said Francis. "And my sister got me out…"

Marguerite was amused at the memory.

They shared some bread, cheese, and wine.

"Are you having a good day?" Rabelais asked the Teacher amiably.

"The kids read 'The Hare and The Tortoise.' That was fun. Then I haggled with two farmers about the price of artichokes."

"Do you grow artichokes here?"

"Whole fields of them."

"I love artichokes," Rabelais chortled.

"How are the bastides governed?" Calvin cut to the chase.

"A council of elders is elected by popular vote," Xita responded. "I'm an elected elder."

"Women are on the council," Marguerite affirmed.

"Five women and five men," said Iker.

"These bastides are hidden inside the ancient feudal dukedoms and bishoprics," said Francis who had roamed about France and visited quite a few bastides.

"In spite of feudal special privileges, the people do matter," said Xita. "Their opinions need to be heard."

Ironically, it was King Francis who asserted, "People are quite capable of governing themselves."

"They are indeed," agreed Iker the teacher. "It would seem that our King is a democrat!"

"Right under the nose of noisy nobles," Rabelais alliterated using his deep voice to good effect.

"Who presides at the council of elders?" Calvin continued his questions.

"I do," responded Iker. "That is part of my Teacher's job description."

"So…?"

"I chair the meeting. I give my opinion. I'm not allowed to vote."

"Well that's a fine how-do-you-do!" Rabelais snorted.

"I do the voting," Xita laughed.

"Is there a chain of command among teachers?" Calvin asked.

"How do you mean?"

"Pope down to cardinal down to bishop down to priest."

"No hierarchy. Teachers have parity."

"What's parity?" asked Rabelais.

"Teachers have equal standing with each other at Colloquies."

"Colloquies? What's that?"

"Colloquies are regional meetings. One elder and one teacher represent each bastide. Then… I get to vote. We act as a regional authority."

"Are there women?" asked Marguerite.

"Yes. Women make the best elders and teachers."

"In your opinion?"

"In my opinion. My wife is an excellent elder here."

Rabelais raised his throaty voice. "Let's drink to women elders!"

Beyond the market stalls, people were playing Pétanque. "We have a foursome," said Francis.

"Let's make it a six-some and include Iker and Xita," said Rabelais.

Word got around the bastide that the King was here and playing Pétanque. Soon a crowd collected and the marketplace became a tournament grounds. Francis loved to play the King. Francis put on a hat that made him like a Gallic chieftain. Then his sister tossed her boule and knocked him off the jack. The village roared with laughter along with their King!

The market had some Indian popping corn from New France brought back by the explorers. They all sat down around a big bowl of popcorn. Soon, Rabelais strode off to get more. Francis took off his Gallic hat.

"A Gallic cashel has a lot of bastide features," said Iker the Teacher.

"Go on," Francis leaned forward. "France used to be Gaul."

"Gallic cashels were a small self-contained village."

"Self contained?"

"The Gaul's didn't trade much. Only their intelligentsia traveled—the bards, the wrights, and the druids."

"Please explain."

"A wright would visit and show how to make the latest mouse trap."

Rabelais laughed. "Bards visited and told the latest jokes!"

"Let's pursue this Gallic Law," suggested Marguerite.

"The Gaul's were accepting people. They included the stranger."

"The Gallic Church accepted outsiders, pagans, agnostics, and others simply because they were human beings," said Rabelais. "When I lived in Lyon, a very Gallic city, I learned that love was important, not sin and guilt. If a single girl became pregnant, she and her family were not disgraced."

"Under Gallic Law, there are no bastards," added Calvin. "All babies were christened before the community as children of God."

"Similarly," Rabelais went on. "Everybody got an honorable burial. Nobody was buried outside the fence."

"Under Gallic Law, Christians, Jews, Moors, Pagans could intermarry."

"This has been a most enlightening day," said King Francis. "Would you draw up a draft of our new form of government that we've discussed?" he looked at Calvin. "Put your head together with Pierre de l'Estoile and come up with a draft."

Then without further adieu, Francis mounted his white stallion and was off in a cloud of dust. His Scots guards came out of the crowd and followed with all deliberate speed.

"La farce est finie. Je vais chercher le vaste peut-être."

"The farce is finished. I go to seek the vast perhaps."

—François Rabelais

...the bastide council of elders...

Iker the Teacher of the bastide watched the King ride off on his white stallion and then he approached Queen Marguerite, Rabelais and Calvin.

"I have a meeting of the council of elders right away. Perhaps you would like to sit in."

"What a marvelous opportunity," said Queen Marguerite.

"I'm game," chimed in Rabelais.

"This may provide the draft of our new form of government," Calvin weighed in.

The elders sat in a half circle of chairs under the arboretum. The Iker the Teacher stood at a portable lectern. "We have three guests, the Teacher began—our Duchess of Berry, François Rabelais and Jean Calvin."

The five women and five men rose, bowed, and sat down again. It was obvious that Marguerite had been there before. They seemed familiar to each other.

"*The first item* is the price of artichokes. As you know a half-bushel of artichokes are measured out for every one of our sixty houses. It's the remaining artichokes we sell." The recording clerk said, "Would you all scribble a price on a parchment and we'll take the average for the price? Put them in this box."

"*The second matter* concerns the damages caused by the Bishop and his hunting party to our farms and gardens. A Berry Colloquy of our ten bastides is called for tomorrow—a Teacher and an Elder from each. The Colloquy Tribune will preside and carry out directives. She is sacrosanct like a Roman Tribune—the Colloquy will protect her at all costs."

"It is proposed that Tribune Adéle present a fine to the Bishop of 1000 gold ducats. The gold will be deposited in the Berry Colloquy Credit Union. If the gold is not received in three days, the Colloquy Compagnons du Berry will withdraw from work on the Cathedral—windows, gargoyles, moldings, etc. All worktables will be removed until further notice. The Compagnons will move on to their next job." The Teacher looked around.

A hand went up, "Are the Compagnons all up to doing this?"

"Their foreman indicates they are."

"How about Tribune Adéle? Can she talk up to the Bishop?"

"The Compagnons are going with her. If anyone lays a finger on Tribune Adéle…"

"*The third issue* is a Bourges Colloquy proposal to go to the General Assembly of France. Based on the model of the new Collège de France, it is proposed that all Colloquies across France each have a public humanist secular university free to all achieving students of the Bastides."

"What an incredible meeting!" exclaimed Rabelais.

"Our dream is already happening," agreed Marguerite beaming.

"The Teacher handed me documents of the Bastide/Colloquy system," said Calvin. I'll meet with Pierre de l'Estoile to draft it up legally."

It was mid-afternoon when they parted. Marguerite and her entourage were returning to Chateau Clos Lucé to be with her daughter, Jeanne. Rabelais planned to go to Coligny to meet up with Jean du Bellay.

Calvin got a parchment from his pouch and scribbled some notes. He ran them past Iker and Xita who added a few items. He thanked the Teacher and took a wistful final mental survey of this most human bastide.

Francis had allocated him a roan stallion to ride. He trotted through the gates in earthen wall and out along the Cher. Willows grew along the green banks. He looked back with fondness at the treed settlement that was Villeneuve-sur-Cher evaporating behind him in a mythic mist. The roan made the seven miles back to Bourges a pleasure. Impromptu he was whistling the chanson—*Sur le Pont d'Avignon*—as he crossed the bridge into Bourges.

Jean Calvin took a corner table in the café of the Royal Arms. He was happy and hungry. With a flush in her face, Brigitte came to his table and presented him with a ploughman's plate.
"You look hungry," she said and filled his wine glass.
"I am," Jean looked up into her eyes.
Later she poured a second glass of wine. She leaned forward, "I have a nicer place for us tonight. I'll be off work in a half an hour."

With anticipation, he sat back, sipped his wine, and watched her move around the tables of the café. Then she was gone...
He muttered aloud a line from Ovid—
"What is it the heart does....? Without it, one only sleeps..."
A voice behind him said—
"With it alone, one lives..."
And then she was gone again.

When she finished work, she came with a cape over her shoulders.

"Let's go for a walk," she said.

They walked out of the café and turned towards the University. They circled the flowered path around quadrangle.

"*Quos amor verus tenuit, tenebit*," Brigitte took his hand.

"True love will hold on… to those whom it has held," he translated and looked at her. Then he quickly broke the spell. "That doesn't sound like Ovid."

"It isn't. It's Seneca."

"Seneca?"

"Aren't you a Seneca scholar? That's what you told the Duchess."

Jean was at a loss, "Do you know? I've never bandied words with a girl before."

"You haven't? Not even at school?"

"I've only spoken to my mother and Queen Marguerite," he admitted. "There were never any girls at my schools. Only boys and priests."

"So…you've never touched a girl?"

"Touched?"

"Like this…" Brigitte lightly touched his hand.

Jean shivered, "My mother gave me a hug a long time ago."

"That's it?"

"Well…you snuggled next to me in that cramped bay window…"

Brigitte squeezed his hand that she was still holding.

Jean squeezed back, "All I could think about today was your warmth close to me last night."

"I thought you were talking tall thoughts to King Francis?"

"Well…yes…but all the time I was thinking of you."

"We didn't do anything…" she said. "We just kept each other warm like a couple of kittens."

"*Quos amor verus tenuit…*" he whispered.

In the morning, Brigitte and Jean had breakfast together in the café.

"I want to revisit Villeneuve-sur-Cher," he said. "Would you like to ride out there with me?"

"This 'bastide' phenomena has you thinking?" she quizzed.

"It does. The bastide is the model for what I have to write for the King."

"Okay. And then let's visit my parents."

"Your parents…?" he took a long breath.

She laughed. "It's not what you think! My parents are compagnons. I grew up in a bastide of compagnons—the Colloquy Compagnons du Berry."

Jean tilted back on his chair and spilled his coffee and Brigitte laughed.

"Did you know that your parents are boycotting the Bishop?" he asked.

Then she really laughed.

Jean was mastering things he hadn't picked up in Law College.

They walked to the livery where the roan stallion was brushed and waiting.

"Shall I try to get a second horse?" he felt her out.

"The stallion is big and strong," she laughed. "Let's ride together."

She had fathomed his feelings.

The livery had a mounting step. Brigitte stepped up and threw her peasant dress over to straddle the horse. Adjusting her skirt under her, she looked at Jean to mount behind her. Then they trotted out of Bourges.

"Have you been to Villeneuve-sur-Cher?" he asked.

"When I was a little girl, the Compagnons rebuilt that bastide. A hunting party of the nobility had set the place afire for sport. So the other bastides in the Berry Colloquy rallied to rebuild Villeneuve-sur-Cher. That's where the Colloquy Compagnons du Berry were brought in."

Jean was absolutely amazed.

At Villeneuve-sur-Cher, they completely circled the bastide. Jean wanted to explore the territory. At the gate, he dismounted and helped her down off the stallion. They had a brief exhilarating embrace.

They walked with the horse through the berm and followed the path inside the palisade around the perimeter. At the market, they split an apple and ordered an assiette aux fromages with fresh bread. It turned out to be a great variety of cheeses including Roquefort. A carafe of local wine completed their meal.

"How did you come by Roquefort cheese?" Jean asked the waiter.

"One of our villagers came from Caves Roquefort just yesterday. It's really a delicacy."

"Have you been to the Caves Roquefort?" Brigitte asked Jean.

"No. Have you?"

"Yes, with the Compagnons. We were there for a month stabilizing the posts in the cave and rebuilding shelves for the fermenting cheese."

"Did you watch them make cheese?"

"They poke a special fungus into the cheese. The milk comes from goats that are found only near Millau."

The waiter brought another small plate of Roquefort cheese with another loaf of French bread.

"The furthest south I've been is Cahors," Jean spoke.

"Clement Marot grew up in Cahors," said Brigitte. "There's

a marvelous medieval walking bridge there. It's the symbol of the town."

"Do you know his poetry," Jean asked her.

She responded:

> *Adieu, bright eyes, that were my heaven!*
> *Adieu, soft cheek, where summer blooms!*
> *Adieu, fair form, earth's pattern given,*
> *Which Love inhabits and illumes!*

"When I was in school with boys and priests, love poetry made no sense," Jean said.

"So..." Brigitte looked into his eyes. "Is it beginning to make sense now?"

Jean smiled.

Brigitte changed the subject. "My parents and their fellow compagnons are boycotting the Bishop for how he and his hunting guests trashed these gardens."

"But look at the gardens now. Les paysans have completely restored the plants and soil. They turned the other cheek."

"What do you mean by that?" queried Brigitte.

"It's a teaching of Jesus. He said, "If a bully strikes you on one cheek, turn and let him strike you on the other."

"Jesus said that?"

"Yeah... look at these fields. It seems to work."

She eyed him and smiled. Brigitte liked this fellow but he had a lot of quirks and baggage.

"So I'm the first girl you've ever had a conversation with?"

Jean looked up from the remaining cheese. "I was in Catholic boys' schools. Girls were not allowed. Priests were abusive."

"That's terrible," Brigitte reacted. "My bastide school was gentle."

"How were the priests abusive?"

"You don't really want to know do you?"

"You mean… that way?"
"Yeah. That way."
"The Church won't let them have wives?"
"Celibacy. It's a big lie."

Brigitte asked, "So being with me is like breaking the rules?"
"Not any more. I like being with you. I like talking with you. I don't think I can tolerate the thought of not being able to talk with you."
Brigitte looked deeply into Jean's eyes without saying anything.
"You even talk to me with your eyes," he said.

"You put me in front of you on the stallion…"
"Did you want to ride behind me?"
"No… I liked it. It seemed natural. But I could feel…"
He put his hands over his eyes.
"I'm sorry. Priests say that natural things like that are bad."
"I felt it as a compliment," she laughed fondly and touched his hand.
"I'm carrying a lot of unnecessary baggage in my head," Jean said.
Brigitte smiled affectionately. "I think you are getting rid of a lot of baggage."
"When my father died, I broke free of the church…"
"I'm discerning what you are saying," she said.
"I wanted to become a humanist lawyer."
"A humanist lawyer?"
"Human law for daily life. Church law can tie you in knots."
"In your humanist mind you're learning to be human…"
"Right. I read Ovid. I translated his Love Poetry. But I had no idea…"

This time she reached across the table with both hands and grasped his.

"Brigitte, you are the most human person I've ever met…"

They rode back to Bourges. She sat behind him on the stallion and held him tightly.

Brigitte's parents regarded Jean Calvin attentively when they rode up. They were seated together in their garden. They got up and came forward.

Jean dismounted and helped Brigitte get down.

"This is the lawyer that I've told you about," Brigitte began.

"I'm Jean Calvin," he extended his hand to her father.

"Welcome to our habitation," her mother said very cheerfully.

"I'm very impressed with what I've learned about Compagnons," Jean said.

"We think it is a good life for a woman and a man," her father commented.

"My mother specializes in stained glass. My father in architectural art," said Brigitte.

A second lady came forward from their garden retreat.

"Monsieur Calvin, please meet Tribune Adéle—our Colloquy Tribune," said Brigitte's father. "She has just returned from depositing our plebiscite with the Bishop."

"I was apprised of your actions at Villeneuve-sur-Cher," Jean responded. "You have taken a very meaningful and courageous step…"

"You see it as historic?" inquired Tribune Adéle.

"I see it as an act of solidarity on the part of people who were wronged," said Jean.

"The Bishop didn't see it that way."

"It is curious how those who pose as moralists do not understand morality," Jean continued

"The Bishop feigned concern," said Adéle. "He bowed and scraped when I handed him the plebiscite scroll."

"By analogy," Jean responded, "our King is placing the Collège de France on the doorstep of the Sorbonne."

"A true analogy," nodded Tribune Adéle. "A humanist college as plebiscite handed to the Sorbonne patricians."

"Our daughter tells us that you have a similar task," Brigitte's mother entered in.

"King Francis is using your skills to place humanist leaven in the feudal loaf of France," said Brigitte's father.

"I hope the dough rises," Jean laughed with a gentle humor.

"Oh it will!" exclaimed Brigitte.

Jean blushed. Then he said, "Your bastide/colloquy is a ready-made model."

"We think it is," said Adéle.

"I'm meeting with Pierre l'Estoile tomorrow in Orléans to write it up."

Bidding adieu, Jean helped Brigitte mount the stallion. Then he took the reins and led them off to the hotel livery.

"Well aren't you the gallant knight in shining armor," Brigitte spoofed.

"I didn't fancy mounting behind you with a parental audience," Jean laughed.

"Mounting me?"

"I did not say that!"

"I couldn't resist saying that."

"It figures."

"You like my figure?"

She had him spellbound.

"Tomorrow…?" Brigitte suddenly blurted.

"I could go to Orleans this afternoon," Jean smiled teasingly at Brigitte.

After they returned the horse, Brigitte poked his ribs on both sides.

"What's that all about?" he yelped.

They walked the streets to the Bourges Cathedral. Entering, they could hear the organist rehearsing high above them.

"That is a real feat to get to that organ loft," said Brigitte. "My father says that it is a tiny ledge with no railing. It's a hundred feet straight to the Cathedral floor."

"So let's get a guitar instead," Jean talked fast.

"I already have a guitar."

"I'm all ears."

"Not tonight."

"See that broken glass up there above the hammer beam," Brigitte said. "My mother will replace that…eventually."

"Eventually," Jean repeated. "Do you like Picardy beer?"

They found a secluded pub off the Quadrangle.

"I think I prefer rosé wine. It's not so demanding."

"I think I like your feminine mind…"

... ubi solitudinem faciunt, pacem appellant.

"Robbers of the world, having by their universal plunder exhausted the land, the Romans rifle the deep. If the enemy be rich, the Romans are rapacious; if he be poor, they lust for dominion; neither the east nor the west has been able to satisfy them. Alone among men they covet with equal eagerness poverty and riches. To robbery, slaughter, plunder, the Romans give the lying name of empire; they make a solitude and call it peace."

—General Calagacus speech at Mons Graupius

...the proud Vercingétorix...

A walking path saw-toothed down valleys and up ridges between Bourges and Coligny. The journey allowed Rabelais a chance to think about conversations with Queen Marg. He zigzagged beside the Loire for a few miles before reaching his destination. That longest river was halfway from the high wilds of the Ardèche to the Atlantic. At Chinon near his birthplace, the Loire was wide and glorious. Here the Loire was quite narrow.

Rabelais met Cardinal Jean du Bellay at an auberge familiar to them both from earlier travels. They sat in the pub under a relief of a moustached Gaul and two fragments of a Druidic calendar banned by the Romans.

"So...what's the plan?" Jean du Bellay asked his friend.

"Well...our end game is Chateau Clos Lucé," said Rabelais. "But on the way I thought we might visit Vercingétorix at Alésia."

"Since we are contemplating the Gaul's, I heartily agree!" and Jean du Bellay raised his mug of beer.

"What do you know about this Gallic calendar we're sitting under?"

"I think it shows a fantastic understanding of the universe."

"The Keltic intelligentsia?" queried Rabelais.

"You mean the traveling teachers—*druids, bards* and *wrights*..." said Jean du Bellay.

"We know the Gaul's were homebodies. They stayed in their cashels and crannogs. They were forerunners of the bastides," Rabelais commented. "Want another round of beer?"

"Do you consider yourself a traveling teacher? A *druid* of sorts?"

"Never thought of it that way," Rabelais laughed. "I'm a doctor like a *druid*. But I'm also a *bard*. I like to tell funny stories."

"This Gallic calendar...they figure it's a 19-year cycle of the sun and moon, month by month, night and day."

"Incredible," Rabelais drank deeply at the thought. "I heard it starts on Hallow-even!"

"The first of Samonios. That night earth passes close to heaven. It's so close you can wave and say hello to your dead relatives," Jean du Bellay related.

"Is that a good thought?" Rabelais asked tongue in cheek.

"I've been a diplomat and a bishop. I would like to try out being a *druid*..."

"Let's pass Biberacte on the way to Alésia. That way we will visit two capitals of the Gaul's," suggested Rabelais.

"The Aedui at Biberacte and The Mandubii at Alésia," affirmed Jean du Bellay.

"Do you remember when we climbed the heights of Gergovia in the south?" recalled Rabelais.

"Yes. Gergovia was the capital of the Avernii. Vercingétorix soundly defeated Julius Caesar and his bloody Romans at Gergovia."

"I prefer the Romans back in the days of their Republic," Jean du Bellay reflected.

"Why is that?"

"The Plebians had achieved a certain equality of rights with the Patricians."

"Then what happened?"

"The Punic Wars."

"And the Plebians had to go fight whilst the Patricians made money off the wars."

"And after that?"

"The Romans became imperialistic…"

"And their Roman Law lost its savor. It became barbaric…"

They reached the top of Mont Beuvray on a holiday. They climbed up and over an ancient Keltic wall. Stones were strewn everywhere. Inside the summit hillfort of the Aedui, the locals were picnicking and playing Pétanque.

"Do you think these people know about their ancestors?" Rabelais wondered aloud.

"More than you think!" Jean du Bellay asserted. "Your Gallic temperament certainly shows itself on occasion!"

A tall woman with blue eyes and red hair aligned herself to toss a Pétanque boule. The ball looped the loop and came down beside the jack knocking every ball outside the court.

"Did you see that?" Rabelais was amazed.

"No one but God understands her Pétanque logic," said Bishop Jean du Bellay.

The woman turned and glared at the Bishop. Gallic Jean suddenly lost his gall. The tall woman towered above Jean and threw down the gauntlet. She was not someone to be challenged.

"Okay…" Jean managed to squeak.

"Three pops and you give me that fancy bracelet," she wagered.

"What do I get if I win?"

She looked Jean du Bellay up and down. "You won't. You go first."

Jean tossed out the jack about half way along. Then he took an underhand swing and lopped his ball within inches of the jack.

The woman wound up her arm like a spring and looped her steel ball squarely on the jack and ricocheting Jean's ball to the far reaches of time.

Rabelais fell off the fence, he was laughing so hard.

"What's your name?" Rabelais asked the woman.

"Boudicca," she replied. "My ancestor chased the Romans out of Britain."

The same performance was repeated two more times.

"Okay mooncalf, hand over that bracelet."

Jean gave a wistful look at his cherished bracelet and handed it over.

"Let's get out of here before she takes my pantaloons," he muttered.

When they were halfway down the mountain of Biberacte, Jean asked Rabelais, "What's a mooncalf?"

Further along the way down they passed through a dark forest. Suddenly out of the trees a squealing wild boar raced towards them. The two men both climbed nearby trees. Then a growling wolf came down the trail chasing the boar. And off they went.

"Sheesh..." said Jean du Bellay. "That was close!"

"Did you hear about the crazy guy who went to see the doctor?" asked Rabelais with a slight smile.

"What about him?" Jean du Bellay took the bait.

"The crazy guy thinks he's a wolf!" continued Rabelais.

"So what did the doctor tell him?" asked Jean du Bellay.

"The doctor told him, 'Whatever you do, don't let your grandmother visit!'"

The ruins of a Roman town covered the hilltop. Here once

stood Alésia, the Gallic citadelle of the Mandubii. The natural hill of Alésia purveyed wide green valleys on all sides. Rabelais and Jean du Bellay visualized the hill circumvallated with double Roman fences of pointed palings.

Inside these imprisoning fences, Vercingétorix and the Mandubii awaited help from other Gallic tribes—help that never came. In the end the imperial despots tortured the proud Vercingétorix all the way to Rome. In their gladiatorial arena, they paraded the proud Gaul as trophy of war.

The two men walked up the colonnaded street. Once bustling with people, it was all but abandoned.

Perchance, a young woman formed pottery on a wheel in the environs of an ancient kiln.

"Are you firing a Roman kiln?" asked Jean du Bellay.

"Yes. I've tuck pointed the old brickwork to handle my fires."

"Your pottery is quite artistic," Rabelais said. "I like the imaginary faces on the sides."

She put her newly formed pot on a firing tray along with others. Then a baby cried from a small cradle behind them. She picked up the baby, opened her dress and began nursing.

Rabelais picked up a pot from her finished work. "Might I buy this pot?" he asked.

"For sure," she responded. "Not many people come up here."

"So where do you live?" Jean du Bellay pursued her situation.

"I camp here," she said. "The Duke had his way with me and now I'm alone with my child."

"It is obvious that you know pottery," Rabelais assured her.

"My father was a potter…"

"Was?"

"The Duke ransacked my father's shop for sport. He and his friend trashed his shop with their dueling lances. His friend ran my father through and then laughed," the young woman related.

"They are looking for a potter where we are going," Rabelais said.

"Where might that be?" she looked at him directly.

"Chateau Clos Lucé it is called."

"Never heard of it."

"It's a small chateau where Leonardo da Vinci lived."

"Really. My father once took me to Fontainebleau where Leonardo was working. We saw him at a distance through the gates."

"Then you might appreciate potting in Leonardo's old workshop."

Leonardo da Vinci met the young King Francis in Italy. They got on well. Francis invited Leonardo to come to France. He gave Leonardo a salary of 10,000 Italian scudi and the petite Château Clos Lucé.

Leonardo designed stairways and chateaux. He painted. He sculpted. He invented mechanical machines.

On 2 May 1519 Leonardo died at Chateau Clos Lucé. Leonardo and Francis had become close friends. Vasari records that Francis held Leonardo's head in his arms as he died.

A two-wheeled hooded cabriolet sped at a rapid clip around the curved driveway to the Chateau. Jean-Pierre and Helene were drinking a coffee outside in the portico. Queen Marguerite was writing at her window on the second floor with her daughter, Jeanne.

They all curiously watched as Rabelais stepped out of the cabriolet with a swirl of his cape. He helped a young woman with her baby to alight. Jean du Bellay and the driver riding up behind the passenger compartment came down to unload the luggage. The single horse between the upward-curving shafts stood obediently at rest.

...the proud Vercingétorix...

Queen Marguerite was down the stairs and outside in an instance. Jeanne followed behind with great curiosity.

Rabelais was at his pompous best—a man with a mission. He greeted his Queen with a sweeping bow.
"My Gracious Queen..." he began. "May I present Charlotte Pensée and her daughter, Marie Louise?"
Charlotte curtsied with her proud bright eyes looking at the Queen. Charlotte wore a colorful peasant dress with a cape. The coverlet for her baby matched her mother's clothing. It was obvious that the woman was poor but had self-confidence in good taste.
"May I hold your baby?" Jeanne broke the stiffness of the moment.

"Charlotte is an artist," Rabelais began with none of his usual joking around. "She is a potter that Jean du Bellay and I met on the Hill of Alesia."
"I would like to see your work!" Queen Marguerite said softly. And Rabelais produced the pot that he had purchased.
"So..." Rabelais proceeded, "I knew that you were looking for a potter, and Charlotte needed..."
"...a place to be an artist," Marguerite finished his sentence. "Let's visit Leonardo's workshop. Jean-Pierre, would you lead the way?"
The workshop was beneath the chateau. The kitchen and servants' quarters were on the first floor. The upper floor were the rooms now occupied by Marguerite in residence. Her husband, Henry of Navarre stayed mostly in the south at their Chateau at Nerac.
Guy and Luc were in the shop fixing harness. They walked past some of Leonardo's half-finished inventions. The pottery workplace was in the corner with lines of shelves for finished pots. The kiln—a large corbelled beehive—stood outside in the yard to prevent possible fire.

"Leonardo da Vinci worked here…" Charlotte spoke with awe.

"He did indeed," Queen Marguerite affirmed. "I often watched him."

"My father and I watched him at Fontainebleau," Charlotte said. "We looked through the gate."

Marguerite was warming to this young potter. "Do you think you would like to work here?" she asked.

"Most humbly… I think it would be a great honor."

"Heléne, would you show Charlotte the rooms overlooking the kiln where she might live with her baby?"

"May I take care of your baby while you look?" Jeanne asked.

Marguerite would have it no other way than the entire group should eat together outside. Rabelais was his old self again. His apprehensions about bringing Charlotte were over in a most positive way.

"Jean du Bellay and I were chased by a wild boar in a dark forest."

"What did you do?" asked Jeanne transfixed by the tale.

"We climbed trees."

"And then," shuddered Heléne.

"A wolf came down the path growling and chasing the wild boar."

"And you were safe!" Jeanne breathed more freely.

"Right! Did you hear about the clown who went to see the doctor?"

"What about him?" Jeanne took the bait.

"The clown thought he was a wolf!" continued Rabelais.

"The clown thinks himself a wolf!" repeated Luc laughing.

"So what did the doctor tell him?" Jeanne pursued the story.

"The doctor told the clown, 'Whatever you do, don't let your grandmother visit!'"

Marguerite and Heléne went into hysterical laughter.

"I don't get it," said Luc.

"Neither do I," said Jeanne.

"Once upon a time, Little Red Riding Hood met a wolf in the forest..." Jean-Pierre related the Fairy Tale.

"Oh" said Jeanne. "If the clown thinks he's a wolf..."

"Yeah. The wolf ate Little Red Riding Hood's grandmother!" said Luc.

"Oh!" said Jeanne nonplussed at Rabelais who was shaking his head.

But Rabelais plunged ahead with another joke.

The Teacher said: "If I gave you two cats and another two cats, how many would you have?" Johnny answered: "Five."

The Teacher repeated: "Listen carefully... If I gave you two cats, and another two, how many would you have?" "Five."

The Teacher said: "Let me say it differently. If I gave you two apples, and another two, how many apples would you have?" Johnny: "Four."

Teacher smiled: "GOOD! NOW if I gave you two cats, and another two, how many would you have?" Johnny: "Five!"

The Teacher shouted: "Johnny, how do you get FIVE?" Johnny answered: "Because I've already got a silly cat!"

At this joke, Jeanne and Luc joined in the laughter.

"I love those who can smile in trouble, who can gather strength from distress, and grow brave by reflection. 'Tis the business of little minds to shrink, but they whose heart is firm, and whose conscience approves their conduct, will pursue their principles unto death."

—Leonardo da Vinci

...a new form of government...

Pierre de l'Estoile was please to see his protégé return to Orléans.

"How did you find Alciato?" he eyed Calvin curiously to see if there was change in his views since last they talked.

"Alciato affects an Italian superiority."

"He wants an edge?" Pierre curled his lip.

"He would like to keep the upper hand," Calvin admitted.

"I gather from what you're saying that he didn't."

"He's not accustomed to a classroom give and take."

"I suppose you altered all that?" Pierre chuckled.

"The law is about debate, the art of argument," Calvin enunciated with a half smile.

"So…" Pierre urged.

"A courtroom is where formal disputation should be exercised," Calvin defended himself.

"You may find that in my classroom. You might find it in an Orléans Law Court. But, it's doubtful you'll find it in Paris."

"The Sorbonne prelates have an administrative jargon that obfuscates the beauty of existence at every turn…"

"That said, you seem to be optimistic," Pierre poked Calvin in the ribs.

"That's the second poke in the ribs I've had in two days!"

Pierre put on a long face.

"Actually, I'm fired up with enthusiasm," Calvin erupted. "Forget about Alciato. I've been with the King and his sister."

Pierre whistled and backed off his stool. "Go on," he pumped Calvin.

"We met in the centre of a bastide—Villeneuve-sur-Cher."

"A bastide… Why a bastide?"

"You know how King Francis is; he's round and about the countryside. He likes to creep up on ordinary people and then announce that he's the King. Townsfolk and peasants are always astonished. But then they discover that Francis wants to be liked by them. He gets off his horse and talks with them very congenially. He was like that with the peasants in the bastide."

"So where is all this leading?" Pierre was on the case.

"He wants us to draft a new form of government for France. A humanist government."

Pierre de l'Estoile straightened up in astonishment. "That's a tall order."

"He wants it next week—before he inaugurates his humanist Collége de France—a new open free university."

"Impossible…!" Pierre almost swallowed his own words.

"You might say," Calvin ploughed on undeterred, "you might say that his Collége de France idea is like his bastide idea."

"How so?"

"The bastides are little democracies within feudal fiefdoms. The bishops and dukes have the power and glory; but in the meantime the bastides operate undercover for the people."

"I'm following."

"Well, the Sorbonne elite have all the power and glory. But, King Francis' free open university will have all the great humanists coming to speak. There will be no certificates or degrees. It will be like when the Moors first brought the university to Europe;

wanderings scholars would go sit at the feet of a great minds at Cordoba like Jewish Maimonides and Moorish Averroes."

"He'll compete with the Sorbonne, but he won't compete," Pierre skipped along.
"Something like that. No admissions tests. No tuition fees. Just learning."

"So these humanist bastides across France are working undercover—leavening the loaf?
"It's happening!" whooped Calvin. "Democracy is gradually overthrowing feudalism."

Pierre de l'Estoile got off his stool and walked over to the window.
"Well…it's a nice dream," he said. "And you are right about Francis. He curries public favor, he sets up games, he loves parades, he curtails the nobility, he empties prisons, he tweaks the bishops, and he does it all in his grand manner. And now in the twinkling of an eye, he wants a new humanist form of government tout de suite."

Unexpectedly, Queen Marguerite arrived in the doorway. There was something surreal about it—even the dreamlike chamber where she found Pierre de l'Estoile and Calvin.

King Arthur back in 470 brought 10.000 troops from Great Britannia to Little Britannia to ward off the Saxon invasion of the Frankish Kingdom. King Arthur fought his last battle and died here in the Duchy of Berry.

Á propos, Queen Marguerite appeared at the door of the Arthurian Legal Chambre. Without formality, she joined Pierre de l'Estoile and Jean Calvin who were sitting at the Round Table. Out of the Camelotian mist of fantasy, King Arthur might have walked in and taken a seat. Like Knights, the two stood up and bowed. Guinevere-like, Marguerite shushed them with her hands and took a seat at the Table.

"My brother has a dream," she began. "But my brother is often quite unrealistic. To his credit, he's filled the Loire Valley with chateaux. He's formed a brilliant court full of poets and musicians. He travels and glad-hands non-stop."

"Our mother," Marguerite continued, "had the political and diplomatic skills to support her son as his regent. When he went off on his wars, she held the fort. But Louise of Savoy has left us—hardly two years past."

"With all due respect, my Queen," intervened the professor, "you deserve much credit as well. Without a doubt, these very Law Colleges at Orléans and Bourges, the dream of Louis XI, have been brought into being because of your keen mind and tactful involvement."

"Thank you. Your words are very kind and appreciated."

"From what Monsieur Calvin has told me, you seem to have your mother's skills in abundance in dealing with this present project," Pierre de l'Estoile acknowledged.

"So…let's get on with it," urged Marguerite. And she broke the surreal spell.

"The essence of the bastide enterprise is that it works around and under the old medieval Duchies and Church. The Bishop and the Duke trample gardens; then the bastide commoners clean it up and go on with their lives. That is the model," put forth Calvin.

"So we want humanist groups of people in France gradually overpowering the medieval church and state with democracy," Marguerite responded.

"You and your brother have set up the Collège de France a few steps from the medieval Sorbonne. You offer a more liberal, modern curriculum than the narrow scholasticism of the

...a new form of government...

Sorbonne with all its ideologies and isms, dogmas and credos. You are not competing with degrees and certificates. You are bringing in distinguished lecturers like Pierre and Alciato. Students will gravitate to the Collège de France to sit at the feet of the greatest minds."

"Inadvertently, The Collège de France is doing what the bastides are doing. Today, the Sorbonne scholastics can trample your new campus. But, tomorrow you will clean it up and bring in Erasmus to speak."

"So..." Pierre summed it up, "our task is to draft a new form of government for France like the Collège de France, like the bastides."

"We don't want another monarchy," said Marguerite. At that they all laughed.

"We don't want another papal pyramid scheme," said Pierre.

The three walked to the window and stared out at the Loire flowing gently by.

Calvin began. "I can think of three historic examples for what we experienced at the bastide. Rabbinic Judaism is based on a minion of ten families with a teacher. A Gallic cashel is an extended family of about thirty with a teaching elder and some ruling elders. The Sisters of The Common Life have scriptoriums of about twenty women with a mentoring teacher."

"You're going too fast. Let's sort this out," said Pierre.

"Okay..."

"Let's start with the role of women," said Marguerite.

"Jacques Lefevre d'Étaples tells us that Mary of Magdala was probably a rabbi. A woman could be a rabbi in Jesus' day," said Calvin. "Rabbinic Judaism accepted women into conversation with men. Jesus talks more to women than to his male disciples."

"I've always hoped it was something like that," Marguerite expressed.

"So Jacques Lefevre d'Étaples is suggesting that at Magdala by the Sea of Galilee, Mary presided over a minion of ten families. She was their rabbi teacher," Pierre followed the logic.

"Something like that," proffered Calvin.

"Where do you get all this?" quizzed Marguerite.

"From your friend—Jacques Lefevre d'Étaples. He is truly a humanist scholar who uses textual and historical analysis. The Sorbonne scholastics want to burn him at the stake for his biblical opinions about women."

"Really?"

"He is the top humanist in my opinion. He gave us the basic text of the Bible—the textus receptus."

"I thought that was Erasmus?"

"The credit belongs to d'Étaples."

"So… we are formulating that a woman's role is equal with a man's role in our new form of government for France."

"Yes!"

"You like that?"

"It's a breath of fresh air."

"Gallic Law also gives women equality. It even protects their security for twenty years of trial marriage."

"How so?"

"Gallic Law states that a husband pays the bride's father a yearly dowry for twenty years! It insures his daughter's security."

"Astonishing!"

"Gallic leaders were called 'teaching elders'."

"Both men and women?"

"Absolutely."

"Tell me more about the Sisters of The Common Life."

"They deserve the credit for the Renaissance—the rebirth of life and literature and everything that's human."

"You think so?"

"In 1374 these abused women turned things around. They copied ancient manuscripts for bread and board. And in so doing, they became literate. They were actually able to read Jesus' parables and teachings in Aramaic as well as Hellenistic Greek."

"Incredible."

"They collected Jesus' teachings into a little book—*Imitating Jesus*. I gave a copy to Ignatius Loyola and he loved it as a model for the society of Jesus he envisions."

They went for a walk. At an outdoor café beside the Loire, Pierre said, "Let's take that table in the shade."

"We went to the bastide for a number of reasons," Marguerite resumed the demeanor of a Queen.

"I wish I had been there," Pierre regretted.

"Pierre," Marguerite looked him in the eyes, "you were there in the person of your student."

"What are you saying?"

"I wanted to find out if this feisty law student that I first saw in action at Bourges Law College was as good as he let on."

"Please…" said Calvin.

"And by the way, I had read the *Antapologia* this law student wrote defending you against Alciato."

"You did…"

"Let me finish," she curbed him. "I had the opportunity to see this law student appreciate the satirist Rabelais. I saw how this law student contained himself in conversation with my brother."

Calvin was silent…

"Francis and I talked after the bastide experience. Francis can read a person in a second. He has other things in mind for you."

"The project is certainly carte blanche," admitted Pierre. "It appears the real clues will come from you…"

"Perhaps," Marguerite smiled. Francis had his mistresses. He had his dutiful, fruitful wife Claude. He had had his regent Mother of Savoy. But the real female role model in his life, Marguerite knew to be herself. Francis had grown up with Marguerite in Angouleme in the custody not only of their mother but also their father's mistress, Jeanne de Polignac. And they all got along famously. Marguerite acknowledged with a nod that she would provide the real clues. She would pick up the pieces.

When the three were back in the Chamber, Calvin said, "I visualize a diamond."

"A diamond?" Marguerite and Pierre questioned.

"Not top down like the papacy. Not bottoms up like the Peasant's Revolt. Something in the middle shaped like a diamond."

"Okay… go on…"

"At the local level are the people, they elect ruling elders. They select a teaching elder who doesn't vote."

"That checks the power of local priests," commented Pierre.

"But those local ruling elders could take things into their own hands…."

"That's where the diamond middle comes in."

"Explain."

"One ruling elder and one teaching elder from each village vote in regional Colloquy. The Colloquy collectively acts as "the final authority." The Colloquy has regional power to act and direct. The Colloquy holds the deeds to all properties. The Colloquy holds the local groups in check."

"I think I like it," said Pierre. "A couple maverick elders can't sell the local meeting house as real estate."

"Finally, at the top is a General Assembly for all of France. One ruling elder and one teaching elder from each Colloquy will form this top group."

"Won't the General Assembly act like a Pope?"

"No. That's the diamond thing again."

...a new form of government...

"The General Assembly can only recommend legislation that all of the Colloquies have to vote on and approve. These proposals are sent up by a Colloquy to the General Assembly. The General Assembly discusses it nationally. But proposals are sent back to all the Colloquies for approval to become law."

"Let me check the procedure," said Marguerite. "Suppose I have a bright idea that all Frenchmen should wear green berets."

"Okay..."

"I bring it to the local elders. The teaching elder doesn't like the idea, but it's put to a vote and the idea wins."

"So far, so good."

"The ruling elder and the teaching elder go to Colloquy with the green beret idea. The Colloquy votes yes."

"Right on."

"General Assembly likes the idea. They send it back to all the Colloquies across France. A majority of the Colloquies agree to green berets. So then, all Frenchmen are to wear green berets."

"That's about it."

"Some things stay local in Orléans. The Berry Colloquy would organize the County Fair. Going to war with Spain needs General Assembly debate and referral back to the Colloquies," Pierre recapitulated.

"It's the diamond form of governing," Marguerite flashed her smile. "Let's meet the King with the final draft. He will be in Bourges the day after tomorrow."

"Le Seigneur nous a donné une table à laquelle se régaler, pas un autel sur lequel une victime doit être offerte; Il n'a pas consacré des prêtres pour faire des sacrifices, mais des serviteurs pour distribuer la fête sacrée."

"The Lord has given us a table at which to feast, not an altar on which a victim is to be offered; He has not consecrated priests to make sacrifice, but servants to distribute the sacred feast."

—Jean Calvin

...the flavor of a bastide...

Two days later, Calvin was at the livery very early. He mounted his horse and arrived in Bourges in time for lunch. Paper in hand, he prepared to eat and write at his usual table in the corner.

Brigitte came to his table and smiled, "Bread, cheese, a pickled onion, an apple and a glass of red wine?"

He nodded smiling back.

"Will you be staying long?" she quizzed.

"Two nights, maybe three."

"I have a nicer room," she brushed past him.

He spread his papers and began to write. The afternoon sun was waning when he pushed his papers aside.

"I'd like a cup of tea and a pastry."

She brought the food and their eyes met…

The following day, King Francis, Queen Marguerite, Rabelais and Calvin met together in the royal suite.

Francis and Rabelais had become easy-going friends. Rabelais was like having a court jester at the table. He always had a new joke:

> A circus impresario walked into a café. A crowd of people watched the little show. An upside-down pot was on a table. A duck was tap dancing on top of the pot.

The impresario was impressed. He haggled to buy the duck for his circus. They settled for three gold coins for the duck and the pot.

A week later the impresario came back very angry. "Your duck is a fraud! I've been swindled!"

"Why do you say that?" asked the duck's former owner.

"I put the duck on the pot before a whole circus audience."

"And what happened?"

"The damn duck didn't dance a single step!"

"So… Did you light the candle under the pot?"

Francis almost fell off his chair laughing. Marguerite looked askance at her brother but was glad that he was relaxed.

"The devil has all the best lines," she gibed dryly.

Francis straightened up and took charge. "So… Rabelais, we have something to tell you. And we want your opinion. Pierre de l'Estoile and Jean Calvin have been drafting a new form of government for France."

"A committee to replace the king?" asked Rabelais. "I doubt if a committee would find my jokes funny. I'd rather stick with the king."

Francis looked rebuffed.

"I thought you enjoyed our day at the bastide," Marguerite interceded.

"You are thinking of making France like Villeneuve-sur-Cher? Peasants working under the noses of the nobility."

"We threshed a lot of new ideas," Francis spoke defensively. "I asked Calvin to take his notes to Pierre de l'Estoile and draft something."

Marguerite took up the logic. "Francis is founding a new humanist university right under the noses of the Sorbonne. Now, he wants to do the same thing with France."

"A democracy evolving within the monarchy," Francis offered defensively.

Rabelais was persistent. "You, my royal friend, are going to open the floodgates to 'civil liberty.' People can say or write or do what we think."

"That's right," confirmed Marguerite. "Throw open the gates to 'spiritual liberty' as well. Of all people, I thought you would love this, François!"

"We'll be free to follow the promptings of our conscience," mused Rabelais. "Rid ourselves of priests and confessionals. I do. I do. I do!"

Calvin laid the draft before them on the table…

"…humanist local groups all over France led by a teacher. Bastides. Villeneuves. Meetinghouses. Community centers.

"…members of the local group vote but not the teacher. She or he can only try to persuade.

"…one member and the teacher will represent the group at a regional meeting called a Colloquy—a collective authority. One member and one teacher from all the groups of the region.

"…the Colloquy will own any and all properties. No pope or local scalawag can make off with the money

"…women and men shall share equally in all humanist endeavors.

"…a national meeting representing the Colloquies shall take place every two years.

"…any action by the national meeting needs to be ratified by all the Colloquies."

Brigitte appeared.
"Would you like more coffee?"
All nodded.

"It has the flavor of a bastide," commented Francis. "It exists by mutual consent. The individual is respected. The activities of the group are transparent. I like it very much."

"Women and men share equally..." reaffirmed Marguerite. "And I also like it very much."

"I understand you translate a bit of Cicero everyday," Francis said wryly to Calvin.

"Usually...."

"So this political analysis of the Classical World makes you the first democrat in the French Renaissance!" cheered the King.

"But..." Rabelais played devil's advocate, "but some self-appointed 'democrat' could say that we need surveillance of our free and open society..."

"Surveillance is an inquisition into one's privacy and liberty," said Marguerite. "Someone looking over your shoulder leads to distrust."

"Let truth and falsehood grapple..." Calvin responded.

"You're right," asserted Francis. "When the bishops and dukes trample our gardens, we will tidy things up and proceed."

"Democracy is vulnerable," said Rabelais. "Democracy needs lots of cleaning up."

"Whatever happened to your sense of humor?" Marguerite glared at Rabelais.

"I'm with you, My Queen. I'm with you," Rabelais defended himself.

Francis was getting ready to leave. "Our new humanist Collège de France will be instituted in two weeks."

Marguerite added, "Just think...a free and open university with top-notch humanist scholars teaching."

Francis furrowed his eyes at Rabelais. "I need an inauguration speech..."

"Don't look at me," Rabelais protested. "I would have

...the flavor of a bastide...

Gargantua and Pantagruel pissing on truth and falsehood grappling."

Francis shook his head. Then he narrowed in on Calvin. "Can you write a speech with terse, powerful phrases? A speech that rivets the minds of the listeners?"

Calvin shrugged, "I don't know…"

Brigitte interceded with a pot of coffee. "You can do it!" she whispered.

Rabelais piped up, "Francis, you should have heard this fellow Calvin verbally counter punching Alciato. That pompous Italian professor didn't know what hit him!"

"I've lost a spate of wars to the Italians," scowled Francis. "Monsieur Jean Calvin, would you please write the speech?"

And off they all went.

Alone again at the café table, Jean sat and collected his thoughts. From behind the royal draperies, Brigitte brought him a mug of Picardy beer.

"It's just amazing," she said.

"What's amazing?"

"The King of France respects you! And the Duchess falls all over you! And even, Rabelais sings your praises…"

"What about you?" Jean eyed Brigitte looking her up and down.

"You know what I think."

"Do I?"

"Do you want to sleep in that cramped bay window in the anteroom?"

"This speech I'm writing has a price," Jean said to Brigitte watching her dress the next morning.

"How do you mean?"

"The King wanted the famous Erasmus to be Chancellor of

his new university. Erasmus was afraid for his life. Erasmus was afraid to come to Paris."

"So what's that got to do with you?"

"The King appointed a figurehead—Nicholas Cop. If things don't go well, Cop will take the fall, not the King.

"The new Chancellor will be the sacrificial lamb…"

"The King will look the other way…"

"And his speechwriter?"

"The King will not be there to pick up the pieces."

"So what do you mean?" Brigitte was forming an ominous picture in her mind.

"The Sorbonne Inquisitors will be there. Their goons will have stakes erected. The firewood will be ready to be ignited. And there will be a quick justice."

"Justice? You mean that you and Cop will burn?"

"My only hope will be Queen Marguerite. She makes France work, not her brother. But they are after her as well."

Brigitte crawled back on top of Jean and held him tightly.

"If I escape, where could I hide? Not Orléans. Not Bourges."

"Villeneuve-sur-Cher," Brigitte proposed.

"Now that is possible," Jean mulled it over in his mind.

"Villeneuve-sur-Cher has small habitats for teamsters, compagnons, and travelers."

"I will have to play cat and mouse with the Inquisitors. It will take some doing to find my way back to Villeneuve-sur-Cher."

"And I can be with you."

"The speech is on All Hallows' Day, 1 November 1533."

"Our habitat will be ready and waiting."

An excerpt from *The Inquisitor*, a play by Marguerite de Navarre

>Times are getting forever worse
>Religion is of no account.
>Our prestige, and this I much lament,
>May too soon wane and bring us shame
>This new knowledge eclipsing ours
>Will rob us of honor and fame,
>And thus I must, from the pulpit,
>Speak each day till I destroy it.
>Were I only dealing with the ignorant,
>I would frighten them back into the fold;
>"Tis the scholars than I cannot silence,
>For better then I they know Holy Writ
>No longer can I content them by feint;
>Forever they seem to quote the Scriptures,
>Which had truly never read with care,
>And thus, much pain and toil I must endure.
>Learned theologians of the Sorbonne
>Many year ago made me a doctor.
>Four years now a Great Inquisitor
>Of our faith, I have indeed spared none.
>I shall not say that when I am offered
>For a man's life a substantial sum
>But let not a word of this be whispered!
>I am promptly willing to save him,
>But a fool will allow himself to die:
>I can provide against him a witness,
>Yet he refused to pay for his life,
>As reason and common sense would suggest
>Although I see no reward in his death.
>He will still burn in the fire of Hell,
>But should he irritate my aching brain,
>I shall think naught of burning him alive.

...a sad, horrendous day...

"This is a sad, horrendous day," whispered Rabelais to Jean du Bellay. "They want to burn our friends at the stake." He stood helplessly at the edge of the noisy crowd powerless to do anything. His usual mirth was gone…

The dark windows of the aging scholastic fortress looked down on the foreboding events coming about in the public plaza below. From the upper balconies, Sorbonne theologians mixed with Parlement justices shrewdly calculated their war against the crown. Their Inquisition was present in full force and casting a dark shadow. The sins of the guilty must be burned. Three tall stakes stood in pyres of combustible sticks ready to be ignited. The Prosecutor encouraged his hired thugs to agitate the ruffians gathered from the sewers of Paris. Across the way on the Louvre steps of the royal residence, butlers and maids stood wringing their hands and watching—unable to serve in the moment of crisis. Catherine de' Medici curled her lip from an upstairs window. At the Collège de Montaigu, Jean Calvin was hiding out in his old room with Ignatius Loyola.

Deliberately and dramatically, the Sorbonne Inquisitors led the King's sister, the King's valet de chambre, and the King's printer to the place of judgment. A raised platform put the arrested victims slightly above the unscrupulous hooligans—jostling and yelling.

"You are accused of heresy, Queen Marguerite of Navarre."

"For what?" she quietly asked the sullen Prosecutor.

"For your poem, *Miroir de l'âme pécheresse*. What have you to say?"

"Louise of Savoy was the mother of the King and my mother. Of late, she died. The *Miroir* is my eulogy to her."

The testy Prosecutor turned to the second heretic.

"You are accused of heresy, Clément Marot," he sniveled.

"What crime have I committed?" asked Marot the poet laureate.

"You translated the Sixth Psalm from Hebrew to French. Only priests are allowed to translate and interpret the Bible."

"But...my Psalm was lyric poetry requested by the King," Marot pleaded.

"No matter... You have transgressed the Law of God!" bellowed the Prosecutor running out of patience.

"I paid tribute to Louise of Savoy with this Psalm of David. The Psalm is my eulogy to this gracious Queen Mother of France."

"But you are not a priest. And you translated it into French, not Latin. Ordinary people should not be allowed to read the Bible. Only the priests!"

"All my lyrics are in the French language," Marot appealed.

The Prosecutor's eyes pierced Marot with derision and scorn.

Rabelais muttered to Jean du Bellay sarcastically, "Marot is lyricizing all 150 Hebrew Psalms into French chansons. This Prosecutor is a stupid oaf."

"Furthermore," the Prosecutor accused with loathing, "in *L'Enfer* you satirized papal justice."

"Not so..." retaliated Marot.

But the Prosecutor droned on, "When you were in prison, you attacked a guard and helped a prisoner escape."

"That's not the whole story..." Marot protested.

"And…" the Prosecutor was climaxing, "Most odious of all, you were arrested for eating meat during Lent…"

"…eating meat during Lent!" Rabelais repeated and laughed out loud. But the paid hooligans drowned out his ironic laughter.

The Prosecutor flared. He straightened his shoulders. He assured himself that he was quite up to his official task. He called for the royal printer to be brought forward. In the hierarchy of social classes, the printer was at the bottom. The foreboding Prosecutor had a sure victim.

"You are accused of heresy, Antoine Augereau, for printing these heretical documents. What do you have to say?"

"I am honored as the royal printer to be asked to print these memorials to the late Louise of Savoy, our Queen Mother—and mother of our King."

The Prosecutor was not diverted from his objective. The contemptuous Sorbonne theologians and justices looked down impatiently on the three heretics. They wanted it to be over and done with. Unrest was seething across the lands of France. Respect for the nobility and the church needed to be restored. In his off-key monotone, the Chief Justice howled out, "Burn them!" Rabelais looked up at the balcony with scorn. Beside him, a cowled monk shouted, "Sew her in a sack and throw her into the Seine."

Rabelais looked at Jean du Bellay and shrugged. "If I can get out of Paris, I'm going back south to practice medicine."

"Your patient's will be cured by listening to your jokes," Jean responded.

"My book, *Gargantua and Pantagruel*, is doing well, but I can't imagine those Sorbonne geeks up there will tolerate my satire for long."

"I'll look after your publishing interests," Jean assured Rabelais.

Not wanting to watch the execution, they took a long last look at the scene. Then they escaped through the din and clamor of the crowd...

The sound horses hooves and marching boots reverberated down the cobblestone streets. At the head, the royal carriage rumbled into view. The royal Scots' Guard surrounded the scene. His arms raised, the Prosecutor was held at sword's point.

King Francis alighted and went immediately to his sister. Then he escorted her and Clement Marot back to the royal carriage and sent them away.

Then the King looked up at the Sorbonne theologians and Parlement justices.

"Most humbly, I would ask you to rescind your condemnation of Queen Marguerite of Navarre's eulogy—*Miroir de l'âme pécheresse*, and the eulogy of my Valet de Chambre, Clement Marot. Please take these off your blacklist."

"And what do we get in return?" the Chief Justice asked.

To solicit the goodwill of the Sorbonne and Parlement, the King paced back and forth beside the formidable stakes on the pyres. Then Francis did his predictable political waffling. In the pecking order, the printer was dispensable.

The Prosecutor, regally cowed, stood down....

...but poor Antoine Augereau was hanged.

Quand'io son tutto vòlto in quella parte
ove'l bel viso di madonna luce,
et m'è rimasa nel pensier la luce
che m'arde e strugge dentro a parte a parte…

When all of me is drawn in the direction
of that place where my lady's sweet face shines,
and in my thought there shines the lingering light
that burns and melts me inside bit by bit…

—Clément Marot

...our greatest poet...

The royal carriage moved quickly out of Paris and traveled south to Montargis along a zigzagging route to avoid pursuit. Queen Marguerite and Clément Marot sat silently in a state of shock. Their reprieve had come none too soon. They had looked into the face of death…

Renée de France was the younger sister of Queen Claude—wife of King Francis. By her marriage, she became Duchessa di Ferrara in Italy. As Duchess of Chartres, she retained a residence in France at Montargis.

From the royal carriage, Queen Marguerite and Clément Marot saw the Chateau in the distance rising above the village of Montargis.

"How are you feeling by now?" Marguerite asked Marot. He was slouched in his seat.

"I'm okay. Thanks to your brother, we are alive. I am very grateful to be here with you," Marot responded.

"Look my friend, you need to get over it. You need to buck up. You are Francis' valet de chambre. Your write his letters."

"No matter. That just annoys the unlettered of the Sorbonne. They will get me sooner or later like our printer…"

"Now look here! You are our greatest poet!" said Marguerite.

"Brace up! We're almost there! You've got to get your head on straight. You need to look sharp for Renée. Don't let us down!"

A few reflective moments passed. Marguerite looked at Marot and spoke softly: "I like your lyrics. They light up my life."

Marot smiled a thank you. "Ordinary people are singing the Psalms to French tunes," he mused. "That was my goal…"

"Some of your tunes come from interesting places…"

"So…?" Marot looked bewildered.

"The 23rd Psalm to a French cabaret tune…"

"Isn't the cabaret part of God's world?"

"I love it." She kissed him on the cheek.

But Marot couldn't forget. "The Sorbonne indoctrinates ignorance," he declared. "They want to dumb down French society. They want France to be compliant with the Church and the Nobility as it as been for a thousand years,"

"Every day they pile up sticks…" Marguerite echoed. "Until the pyre is torched under the latest heretic. But we can't give in…"

"Francis' daughter-in-law, Catherine is a sly one," Marot revealed. "She butters me up with flattery. But I wouldn't trust her for a minute."

"I agree that Catherine exploits every breach," said Marguerite. "I wonder where she was today?"

They looked out to see gentle doves resting motionless in a line on a fence. They all faced the same way. Little breezes ruffled their feathers.

"The Sorbonne priests would like us to be docile like those doves," Marot commented.

The horses' hooves clopped on the cobblestones of Montargis. The driver pulled their reins to the right and the carriage veered up a winding narrow lane. House roofs leaned out over the street. Hanging flowerpots reached out to almost touch the royal coach.

From the tightly fitted houses of the town, suddenly a spacious landscape opened up on acres and acres. The tall white stone castle stood like a sentinel soldier on alert and keeping watch. Trees and moats and ornate fences did not crowd the high structure. With a certain simplicity, its bleached, ghostlike towers and turrets overlooked green meadows.

The driveway drew a wide circle that dramatized the arrival of stately royal carriages pulled by well-groomed horses with silver-like harness trappings.

Chateau Montargis was the royal residence of Duchess Renée de France. When the entourage halted, Marguerite stepped down into the sunlight and her spirit brightened. She took Marot's arm and they made their way to the stately door.

Perched on a grassy summit overlooking the town, the Chateau appeared incredibly tall. The interior had the same feeling of height. Renée de France descended the winding stairway. With cheerful restraint, she approached her guests knowing only partially the ordeal that they had just endured. But she could read their eyes.

Marot took off his hat. As a male, and especially as a poet, the beauty of Queen Marguerite of Navarre always entranced Clément Marot. Now a second great lady held him spellbound.

"Renée de France, my good friend, please meet Clément Marot, poet laureate of France."

Marot bowed low. The Duchess put out her hand. Marot quickly placed a kiss on her glove. And then he stood silently…

Renée broke the rarefied silence. "You compose poetry…?"

Marot blinked. For a moment he forgot about the events in Paris. Then he reached out for her hand again and spoke:

> "*Beautiful Woman, silent I rise to thee…*
> *From a road less traveled, if you pass by me…*"

Marguerite stepped back quite astonished... She had hoped that Marot would get over their ordeal. Her pep talk must have helped...

Renée was visibly moved. "I was not expecting lines so lovely... Thank you."

"Thank you, Renée," Marguerite interposed. "We have come through quite an ordeal today—Marot and I were facing death... His poetry has turned something very negative into something altogether positive..."

With a look of sympathy, Renée nodded and led them into her library.

Marguerite brought Renée up to date. She carefully detailed the events of their arrest and trial by the Sorbonne Inquisition. Renée could visualize the three standing before the Prosecutor.

"Then we heard the King's carriage and the marching of the Scots Guard," Marot acknowledged with gratitude. "The Inquisition was ready to light the fires."

"My home in Italy has become a place of refuge for many humanists. And now, in my own family, you have become refugees."

"We haven't discussed it," Marguerite said, coming to terms with the situation, "but I think you, Clement Marot, need to flee from France with Renée to her home in Ferrara, Italy."

"I offer you my unconditional invitation to come to Ferrara!" Renée affirmed. "You will be amongst humanist friends. You will be free to compose your lyrics without worry of harm."

Marot shrank back on the cushions. "Is this what King Francis wants?"

Marguerite weighed in. "Francis doesn't know what he wants. I think that you need to be out of here. Francis is playing politics with the Sorbonne. Today, without much thought, he sacrificed Antoine Augereau his printer as a political expediency."

"I also know my sister's husband," Renée avowed. "You might be his next political sacrifice…"

"…if you are around and available!" Marguerite despaired.

"My sister Claude is married to Francis. I can bear witness to the fact that Francis vacillates like a pendulum. Today Francis hunts. Tonight Francis womanizes. Tomorrow Francis acquires a chateau. Tomorrow night Francis parties in Paris."

"In his regal danse macabre, Francis has a short-term memory," Marguerite summed it up succinctly. She had watched her brother swing and sway with whatever way the wind was blowing. Today they had been lucky, but not Antoine Augereau…

The two royal women were of one mind. It was imperative that Clément Marot leave immediately with Duchess Renée for Italy.

"Our mother, Louise of Savoy used to plot the long-term strategy," said Marguerite. "As regent, she sent Francis off to win back northern Italy. And he did it! He won one big battle and then it all went to his head."

"But who determines the game plan now?" Renée prodded but wanting to hear Marguerite affirm herself.

Marguerite locked eye to eye with Renée.

"I do."

Clément Marot appreciated Marguerite with new understanding,

Psalm 7 in the lyrical Psalter of Clément Marot

VII Pseaulme Septiesme
        à ung verset pour couplet à chanter
        Domine Deus meus in te speravi.

Mon Dieu, j'ay en toy esperance:
Donne moy donc saulve asseurance
De tant d'ennemys inhumains,
Et fays, que ne tombe en leurs mains:

Affin que leur chef ne me gripe,
Et ne me desrompe, et dissipe,
Ainsi qu'ung Lyon devorant,
Sans que nul me soit secourant.

O Lord, my God, in thee do I take refuge;
save me from all my pursuers, and deliver me,
lest like a lion they rend me,
dragging me away, with none to rescue. Psalm 7: 1-2

...poet laureate of France in asbstentia...

The next morning before the departures of Renée de France and Clément Marot for Ferrara in Italy, and Queen Marguerite for her return to Paris, a parting ceremony took place in the library of Chateau Montargis.

Queen Marguerite seized a closed parasol like a sword. "Let me play the Jester…"
Renée and Clément Marot looked on in astonishment.
"I knight you," Marguerite faltered unsteadily, "I knight you poet laureate of France *in asbstentia*."
This dramatic tragicomedy moved Marguerite and Marot to tears.
"…*in asbstentia*," he sobbed feeling the touch of the parasol on his shoulders.
In this faltering moment, Renée took charge of the investiture.
"I am Renata di Francia, Duchessa di Ferrara," she regally asserted.
Marguerite and Marot bowed their assent silently.
"My court at Ferrara is now a refuge for French humanists and a meeting place for liberal thinkers."
"To Ferrara…" Marot raised an imaginary glass and pondered the future.

"To your great work translating the Hebrew Psalms…" continued Renée.

"To your Psalms in lyrical French to be sung as chansons…"

"To the Dutch and the Scots who also wish to sing the Psalms to your lyrics and tunes…"

"To Antoine Augereau in the heavenly places. May he oversee the printing of your Psalms so that French, Dutch and Scots may sing from your Psalter…"

Marot took the two women in each of his arms and lyricized:

They'll see, if they arrive in time, all lucid,
All loveliness, all regal-mannered days
Bound in two women, mellowed mysteriously;
Then they'll say that my verse is theirs always…

"That's enough of that…" Marguerite choked tears.

The library became amazingly quiet. Marot walked to the window and looked out. Renée picked up a book lying on the desk.

"With a certain jealousy," Marguerite continued, "I'm leaving you with Renée. May you have a safe trip to Italy."

"And what is your itinerary?" Marot suddenly returned to reality.

"I'm off to our new National Library at Fontainebleau to memorialize Antoine Augereau. Then I'll meet with the humanist Group at Meaux to make final plans for our new free humanist university. Then I'll go incognito into Paris to support Chancellor Cop and Jean Calvin, his speechwriter. On All Saints Day, November 1, 1533, King Francis will inaugurate the Collège de France—right under the nose of the medieval Sorbonne."

"Won't you be arrested again?" queried Renée.

"Possibly…."

...poet laureate of France in asbstentia...

"The humanist Collège de France, the National Library at Fontainebleau—these are all really your ideas." Marot's voice trailed off.

And then they parted.

Pseaulme Neufviesme IX lyricized
by Clément Marot

De tout mon cueur t'exalteray
Seigneur, et si racompteray
Toutes tes oeuvres nonpareilles,
Qui sont dignes de grands merveilles.

En toy je me veulx resjouyr,
D'aultre soulas ne veulx jouyr:
O Treshault, je veulx en cantique
Celebrer ton Nom autentique:

I will give thanks to the Lord with my whole heart;
I will tell of all thy wonderful deeds.
I will be glad and exult in thee;
I will sing praise to thy name, O God Most High.

...Antoine Augereau's bound volumes...

Queen Marguerite's carriage rumbled across the old Roman Road between Paris and Dijon. Beyond this crossing point lay the wide, spacious gardens and chateau that Leonardo named Fontainebleau. Louise of Savoy and Leonardo styled the squarish Italianate box architecture in Fontainebleau design. Here at Fontainebleau, Queen Marguerite engaged Guillaume Budé to develop the National Library of France. Books from various sources were brought together into this new, dry and safe environment for books.

"Geneviève... It's so sad," the two women embraced. Geneviève who managed the Library was placing flowers on the immense oak table near the central desk. A slight woman, she was weeping.

"We were just here with him last week," said Geneviève. "He had just brought in some freshly bound volumes."

"He was so proud of the embossed bindings in gold relief," Marguerite continued.

"Antoine Augereau was such a gentle man," Geneviève sobbed as she adjusted the flowers.

"He was indeed."

"Guillaume Budé our Librarian trusted his judgment more than any other. Budé wanted to show the new books to the King…"

Marguerite shrugged, "I remember it well… Francis arrived, took a cursory glance at the new books, and then saw your latest new damsel dusting books…"

Half laughing and half crying at the thought, Geneviève wriggled a path around the piles of books to be sorted.

"My mother and Leonardo designed this chateau fifteen years ago," Marguerite recalled.

"Louise liked Italian architecture and Leonardo suggested the boxes," said Geneviève. "Fontainebleau looks like a line up of square cake pans."

Slowly walking along, the two women surveyed the fresco paintings above them on the vaulted ceiling of the long library corridor designed by Leonardo. Geneviève eulogized, "Antoine Augereau's bound volumes contributed greatly to the beauty of these shelves beneath the frescoes,"

"The humanism of Lady Wisdom reached her happiest days in these hallowed halls," Marguerite affirmed.

Marguerite's manner abruptly changed. "Geneviève, have you ever entered the Royal Chambre through these doors at the end of the corridor?" Astonished at her change of demeanor, Geneviève protested, "Well, no. It is forbidden."

Taking on her jester role, Marguerite stopped, twisted and bowed to a startled Geneviève. "Mademoiselle Geneviève, let me escort you to the boudoir." In the manner of her foppish brother, Marguerite gripped her arm and guided her through the heavy doors.

"But…"

"Play the role, my Dear Geneviève," Marguerite the Jester commanded.

"Oh Dear! Where are you taking me, My Young Country Swain?"

"To the Royal Bedroom, the better to know you my Dear."

"To KNOW me?"

"In the most biblical sense, my Dear."

They entered the Royal Chambre. Geneviève looked in disbelief. "It's all black as midnight in here!" Geneviève dug in her heels.

"The better to play hide and seek, my Dear," the Jester purred with a low vocal thrum. The walls, ceiling and heavy drapes were all deep dark purple velvet. It was pitch black. Geneviève giggled—enjoying the drama.

At that exact moment, King Francis himself rose up in the velvet blackness. He was lying beside another intimidated damsel in distress. Not a single word was spoken.

Marguerite gripped Geneviève's arm tightly and steered her out of the velvet boudoir darkness and back into the light of the National Library.

The ghost of Antoine Augereau sat at the end of the table patiently handling his newest volumes. A bittersweet Geneviève placed the vase of flowers in front of him. Queen Marguerite curtsied in his direction, then turned and silently left the chateau.

A humanist in Meaux, Bishop Guillaume Briçonnet had been seated ex cathedra by Marguerite. In Rome, Guillaume Briçonnet with Jacques Lefèvre d'Étaples, Bonaventure Des Périers, and Pierre-Robert Olivétan had translated the Bible into French.

The half-finished Romanesque Cathedral in the Marne Valley was an excellent location for the clandestine humanist Group at Meaux. Only 25 miles east of central Paris, Marguerite and Briçonnet decided Meaux was the place to meet secretly. The name Meaux derives from the Gaulic tribe, Meldi. The inhabitants of Meaux are called Meldois.

Founding members of this humanist Group at Meaux included Marguerite, Briçonnet, d'Étaples, Gérard Roussel, Guillaume Farel, Jodocus Clichtove, François Vatable, Martial Mazurier,

Guillaume Budé, Jean du Bellay, Bonaventure Des Périers, and Pierre-Robert Olivétan. All were humanist Classical scholars studying ancient texts of the Greeks, Romans and the Bible.

Originally the Group met at the Cathedral, but Briçonnet had to appear twice before the Paris Parlement on suspicion of heresy. The Sorbonne had charged Jacques Lefèvre d'Étaples with heresy. The Paris Parlement originated as the King's Court in the ancien régime. Now, in these troubled days, the Parlement collaborated with Sorbonne against the crown with their spies everywhere. Since 1525 they met covertly in a backroom of a local pub.

With night drawing nigh, Marguerite had her coachmen drive past the Cathédrale Saint-Étienne de Meaux to a livery. Pulling a cowl over her head, she walked down the dark, narrow street. An exterior lamp guided her to the meeting place.

"Good evening, my Queen," Briçonnet greeted.

"Bon soir my friend. Is everyone here?" asked Marguerite.

"Yes. Guillaume Budé and Jean du Bellay just arrived from Noyon."

A few locals were seated at candle lit tables. At a side table, Jean Calvin and Nicolas Cop were writing the speech for the College de France on the morrow. In the afternoon, Calvin narrowly escaped arrest by the Parlement.

Marguerite and Briçonnet passed through an oaken door at the back. The group was seated around a large oval-shaped table when they entered. With warm welcomes all around, the Queen was a familiar face at their meetings.

"Friends," Queen Marguerite began, "we have met on the eve of the inauguration of our great project."

"A special welcome to Guillaume Budé and Jean du Bellay who pioneered the project," said Briçonnet.

Budé, the National Librarian, spoke with pride. "We have designed the new humanist Collège de France. It will offer a liberal and modern curriculum. It will have a superb faculty of well-known scholars in history, literature, and science."

"All students will be welcome in the Classical tradition of the academic grove," added Jean du Bellay. "Our students will be able to sit at the feet of distinguished lecturers and eminent scholars."

Queen Marguerite took charge with a somber note. "As you may know, Clément Marot and I faced the Sorbonne Prosecutors two days ago. Had not King Francis intervened, we would have been burned at the stake for heresy."

"The Founding Ceremony may be difficult," Briçonnet spoke solemnly.

"Why is that?" asked Budé.

"The Sorbonne and the Parlement may attack the new Chancellor Nicolas Cop as a heretic when he is speaking…"

"I would hope not," said Jean du Bellay. "Our Collège de France deserves a better beginning than that."

"There is a second problem," Briçonnet spoke. "Calvin is here tonight with Cop in the pub. Spies have the word out that Calvin wrote Cop's speech. They may examine him for heresy as well."

"Why were you and Clément Marot charged for heresy?"

"For our eulogies to my mother, Louise of Savoy."

"Eulogies to the Queen Mother! How could that be heresy?" Budé pursued the matter.

"The eulogies had 'humanist' content."

"So what happened?"

As I said, "Francis intervened. Marot and I were able to escape to a safe place. But they hanged Antoine Augereau—the royal printer."

"Antoine Augereau," cried Budé who had just arrived from Noyon. "He has been my constant friend in developing the National Library at Fontainebleau. I can't believe it…"

Their hopes diminished at this news.

Budé was beside himself. "The Sorbonne demanded the King

to prohibit printing in France. Antoine Augereau and I induced Francis to allow printing. Can you believe that?"

"My brother waffled," Marguerite admitted sadly. "He let Antoine Augereau take the rap."

"Thank God that you and Marot escaped," said Briçonnet.

Budé was not to be consoled, "Those dreadful scholastics at the Sorbonne have murdered Antoine Augereau… Those bogus friars are so illiterate they didn't even want a Library."

Marguerite excused herself to go to Calvin and Cop in the pub.

"Guillaume Budé and Jean du Bellay are the notables in the inauguration of the new College du France. Chancellor Cop, I think you should always be with them during your speech and then leave immediately. Come back to Meaux with them," Marguerite asserted.

Cop moved back in his chair and nodded to the Queen.

"I just heard of your narrow escape from the Parlement prosecutors," she said to Calvin. "I think it would not be wise for you to go back into Paris."

Calvin shuffled his papers.

"I mean it Jean. You must leave immediately."

"Bishop Briçonnet wishes to accompany you to Angouleme where Louis du Tillet is Canon of the Cathedral. He has a very large library there," said Marguerite. "You could secretly work there."

"I thank you for the offer. But I would like to return to Villeneuve-sur-Cher," Calvin announced. "Is there a pony in the livery? And maybe a tattered coat and hat?"

"Why Jean?"

"The bastide is safe. Iker, Xita and Brigitte have a loft where I can hide. Later maybe, you'll see me in Angouleme."

Pseaulme Dixiesme X lyricized
by Clément Marot

Dont vient cela, Seigneur, je te supply,
Que loing de nous te tiens, les yeulx couverts?
Te caches tu, pour nous mectre en oubly?
Mesmes au temps, qui est dur, et divers?
Par leur orgueil sont ardants les pervers
A tourmenter l'humble, qui peu se prise:
Fais que sur eulx tombe leur entreprise.

Why dost thou stand afar off, O Lord?
Why dost thou hide thyself in times of trouble?
In arrogance the wicked hotly pursue the poor;
Let them be caught in the schemes which they have devised.

...humanist Collège de France...

In Paris, All Hallows' Day provided the public platform for politicians and parliamentarians, professors and priests. On 1 November 1533, King Francis saw All Hallows' Day as an opportunity to launch his new Collège de France—an opportunity for studia humanitatis in contrast to the ideological. He would endorse his new humanist university with a speech by his newly appointed rector—Nicolas Cop. The new Chancellor was son of Francis' doctor.

Francis had tried in vain to appoint Erasmus to the Chancellor's Chair. Erasmus could talk the talk, but Paris was not a safe place for a Dutch humanist. Erasmus secured himself in Switzerland out of the reach of the Sorbonne Inquisitors.

On 31 October—All Hallows' Eve, the Group at Meaux broke up early to go their various ways.

Dressed in a ragged coat and hat, Jean Calvin headed for the livery behind the Cathedral. He haggled for a white pony from the Camargue that took his eye. He spent considerable time softly talking to the animal and brushing him down. They walked around the enclosure to the watering tank. Then he led the white pony down the dark cobblestone street. Only out of the city did Calvin mount his pony. The animal accepted its new master and they made their way south in the light of a full moon. They did not gallop. They were not in a horse race. They simply cantered along at a steady, easy gait that the pony determined.

The silhouette of Fontainebleau Chateau loomed against the starry sky like a long parapet notched at intervals. In the daylight the place was a spectacle of formal gardens and walks. At night it appeared ominously like an elongated fortress.

The pony's hooves clattered briefly on stones. They crossed over the inexpungible road that Roman soldiers set in place a millennium ago. Then the creature comforting dirt track resumed.

A lamplight welcomed the way to an inn. The innkeeper in a nightshirt pointed the raggedy-coated Calvin to the stable.

"In the stall, there's also a bunk where you can sleep." Enough said.

Calvin led the pony into the stall and closed the gate behind them. The sliding latch reminded him of the bolt in his door at the College Montaigu.

"Intruders beware," he thought to himself.

The pony found some fresh hay in the manger and oats in the grain box.

Calvin pulled an apple from his pouch for himself.

Horses being harnessed in other stalls awakened him. A glorious sunrise began All Hallows' Day of 1 November 1533. The innkeeper brought coffee and a croissant.

By mid-afternoon Calvin was nearing Montargis. A royal coach crossed their path on its way eastward. The driver waved and Calvin waved back. Inside the coach, Duchess Renée of Ferrara and Clément Marot were leaving for Italy. They passed like ships in the night. Calvin was unacquainted with the Duchess or Marot. But the day would come, sooner than later, when he would seek refuge with them in Ferrara.

From the wild highlands of the Ardèche, the Loire was flows north and arcs a wide sweep west towards the Atlantic.

With the setting sun on the glistening waters, they bridged the westward meander of the Loire. Clip-clopping the trestle planks, the pony accelerated down the far side. Two row boats were tied dockside next to an auberge nestled into the south bank. A ramshackle barn offered a leaning shelter. Jean on his pony took a turn around the yard and left.

Looking for something better, they chanced on crannog offshore on the Loire with a narrow causeway. The house on the islet turned out to be a cozy auberge with a shed for horses. They settled in. Tomorrow should bring them to Villeneuve-sur-Cher.

The Berry Colloquy Compagnons halted work on the Bourges Cathedral. The Compagnons took down their ladders, removed their workbenches, and gathered up their tools to go to another job.

Tribune Adéle of the Berry Colloquy had delivered the plebiscite. The Bishop had read the fine for damages caused by his hunting party to the bastide. A hammer-beam, holding up the roof, was slipping off its piedestallo. A stained glass window had shattered—letting in rain. The broken nose of a gargoyle waterspout was flooding the undercroft burial crypts. But now the Bishop was dithering with high-borns who gave final answers.

"Who do these peasants think they are?" asked the blue bloods.

"Who says where we can hunt?" sneezed the upper crusts.

"Have they no sense of our traditions?" snorted a self-appointed amateur historian.

The day before, Tribune Adéle had convened the Berry Colloquy at Villeneuve-sur-Cher.

"It looks like you've fixed the damage," a visiting elder from Orléans commented.

"We were able to replant many artichokes," Iker said. "We had a lot of compost to fill in around the plants."

"It's the principle of the thing," said Tribune Adéle. "The Duke, the Bishop, the nobility who engage in vandalism need a consistent barrage of fines—always the same amount 1000 gold ducats."

"I agree," said a woman elder representing Nevers. "We cannot make an inventory of damages every time and beg for recompense. It needs to be a consistent fine. Eventually they'll get it into their noble noodles."

"In the meantime," Tribune Adéle went on, "we have had a request to assign the Compagnons to refurbish the Chateau at Montargis. The Duchess is away at Ferrara so it is a good time for renovation."

"Duchess Renée is our friend," said Xita. "She provides a place of refuge in Ferrara to many humanists fleeing from the Inquisition in France."

Tribune Adéle added, "Just this week, our Duchess of Berry, Marguerite, faced the Inquisition with Clément Marot, our national poet. They escaped thanks to the intervention of King Francis."

"It is rumored that Duchess Renée is spiriting Marot away to Italy as we speak," the elder from Orléans informed.

"I move that we send the Compagnons to Montargis," the elder continued.

"I second the motion," said the Teacher from Villeneuve-sur-Cher.

"All in favor raise your hands," ordered Tribune Adéle. "All opposed the same. Seeing no opposition, it is carried."

Halfway along from Montargis, Calvin met the wagons of the Berry Compagnons. He recognized the parents of Brigitte, but they did not recognize him in his tattered coat and hat. He hailed the wagon master on a lead horse and the little train halted.

"Were you folks working on the Cathedral at Bourges?" Calvin asked.

"Yes, but the work has stalled because of the Bishop."

"I know about that," Calvin said. "I was at Villeneuve-sur-Cher…"

"Now I recognize you," Brigitte's mother interrupted. "You are the lawyer. You were in danger…"

"It explains my tattered clothes."

Then the caravan moved on to renovate Chateau Montargis.

Spies who think they are invisible are usually the most noticeable. The grapevine of the hotel staff was quietly on alert. Brigitte circled the streets and alleys before taking a pony from the livery stable. Her relationship with Jean Calvin had possibly been noticed. She trotted north towards Orléans along the L'Yévre River before veering west on a treed country path to the bastide. On All Hallow's Eve, she had arranged a hideout for Jean with Iker's help. They chose a vine-covered loft secreted above the end stall in the stable. The horse stall was enclosed with a gate. Behind the manger, a ladder gave access to the loft.

Tonight, she rode into the bastide and tied her horse near the stable water trough. Iker and Xita sat under the arboretum. They invited her to have a bowl of soup with them. Their cottage was next-door.

A foursome of farmers played Pétanque. A group of women were quilting around a large rack. Children played tag in the street. The late afternoon sun warmed the scene.

A stranger appeared in the berm gate riding a white pony. He wore a tattered coat and a rumpled hat. He dismounted and led his pony up the street.

Without fanfare, Iker rose and led Jean to the stable. Brigitte quietly followed. Iker closed the gate of the stall and returned to Xita. The farmers continued their game. The women readjusted their quilting rack. The children, tired of tag, played with their kittens.

Brigitte climbed the ladder to the loft. Jean brushed his pony and fed him some hay and oats. From a bucket, he provided a drink of water. Then he took his pouch up the ladder…

Their close embrace lasted eons and eons. His ominous journey and her unknowing waiting seemed never-ending. Separated from each other, they both were looking back over their shoulders in fear. The five days had weighed like five centuries.

"Do you like this loft?"
"It seems ideal!"
"A place to hide."
"A place to study and write."
"I brought your books and papers."
They embraced again.

"The window was broken and covered over. My mother blew a new glass to size."
"Has she been here?"
"No…she used my measurements. Take a look out."
"It's really a marvelous view of the whole village."
"I met your parents on the road."
"They were traveling with the Compagnons to Montargis."
"In spite of my tattered clothes, your mother recognized me as the lawyer."
"Was she discreet?"
"I think so. The wagon master was in a hurry."
"How much does she know about us?"
Brigitte laughed. "They saw us ride up together on a horse."
"We should have had two horses," said Jean. "It's my fault."
"I don't see it that way. My parents are the best."
"You were riding behind me."

"Maybe it was the way I was holding on to you…"
"She learned everything from that?"
"She looked at the happiness written all over my face."
"The thought of you kept me going," Jean had tears in his eyes.

Pseaulme Unziesme XI lyricized by Clément Marot

Veu que du tout en Dieu mon cueur s'appuye,
Je m'esbahy, comment de vostre mont,
Plustost qu'oyseau dictes que je m'enfuye.

Vray est que l'arc les malings tendu m'ont,
Et sur la corde ont assis leurs sagettes,
Pour contre ceulx, qui de cueur justes sont,
Les descocher, jusques en leurs cachettes.

Mais on verra bien tost à neant mise
L'intention de telz malicieux,
Quel' faulte aussi a le juste commise?

In the Lord I take refuge;
How can you say to me
"Flee like a bird to the mountains?"
For lo, the wicked bend the bow;
they have fitted their arrow to the string,
to shoot in the dark the upright in heart.
If the foundations are destroyed,
What can the righteous do?" Psalm 11:1-3

...the Library of Louis du Tillet...

The Tribunes met at Angoulême. Tribune Adéle of Berry Colloquy called the gathering at the request from Queen Marguerite. Tribunes representing fifteen Colloquies were present. Adéle of Berry, Odile of Burgundy, Nâdiya of Alençon, Héloïse of Anjou, Iseult of Brittany, Irénée of Poitou, Lisette of Guienne, Mireio of Languedoc, Manon of Auvergne, Nâdiya of Champagne, Mathilde of Normandy, Gisèle of Maine, Fleurette of Picardy, Thérèse of Bearn, and Manon of Angoulême. Tribune Adéle of Berry brought her recording secretary, Brigitte.

They met in the Library of Louis du Tillet, humanist canon of Angoulême Cathedral. In his travels, Louis had acquired a rare library of four thousand volumes. Marguerite had secured his appointment in her birth city of Angoulême. She also invited a few other humanists to the meeting of the Tribunes, namely Guillaume Briçonnet, Gérard Roussel, François Rabelais, and Jean Calvin.

"What are you doing here Brigitte?" Jean was pleasantly surprised. He was working in the Library.

"Adele asked me to accompany her and Marguerite as recording secretary."

"So you came from Bourges to Angoulême in the Queen's carriage?" Jean was impressed.

"I had the two best teachers for those two hundred miles. We went by way of the Creuse Valley. It was gorgeous. The Queen said it was her favorite river valley," Brigitte rambled on and on.

Queen Marguerite came into the Library and found Jean and Brigitte chatting.

"I didn't know that you two were acquainted."

"You are responsible," Jean retorted.

"Me?"

"You invited me to supper in Bourges."

"And this intellectual girl?" Marguerite eyed Jean.

"She was keeping her talents hidden by pouring more wine…"

"So that's why…" Marguerite was putting two and two together, "That's why you obeyed so quickly when I told you to not go back to Paris."

"If I had returned to Paris, I would not be here today," Jean replied with seriousness. "I have you to thank."

"So that hideaway you found at Villeneuve-sur-Cher?" the Queen was both serious and amused by her protégé's tragicomedy. "Adéle and Brigitte showed me your hiding place for the last six months. I had a hard time tracking you down."

"The Papists have spies everywhere," Jean defended himself.

"I'll get off your case," she said, "but that hideaway did seem to me to have a feminine touch."

Then she smiled at Brigitte who blushed.

The Chairwoman, Tribune Adéle called the meeting to order with parliamentary rules. With these Tribunes, there was no nonsense. The Tribune tradition began in the days of the Roman Republic. The Roman plebians or commoners had to fight for their rights. The Tribunus plebis took their commoner demands to the Patricians expecting action.

Tribune Adéle recognized Tribune Odile. "I am pleased to

report that the 1000 écu d'or required of the Duke of Burgundy for damages to Bastide-Saint-Germain has been paid."

Tribune Adéle followed up, "Sadly, I must report that the Bishop of Bourges has not paid the 1000 écu d'or—gold coins for damages to Villeneuve-sur-Cher."

Presumptuously and without bothering to address the Chair, Gérard Roussel stood up. His authoritarian scowl swept over women collectively as if he were addressing subordinate nuns. "This meeting of your so-called Tribunes is all well and good, but are you really being helpful when you demand 1000 écu d'or from the Bishop of Bourges? Why don't you back off these silly demands and let the Bishop get back to his work?"

Tribune Adéle pounded the gavel. "Bishop Roussel, the Chair has not recognized you and your comments are out of order."

"But…"

"Bishop Roussel, you are a guest in this chamber with no privileges of the floor. Please sit down."

Shoulders shaking, François Rabelais choked down his laughter. Jean Calvin kept a poker face throughout the scene. Queen Marguerite observed her two protégées with the hint of a smile.

Without a break, Tribune Adéle moved to the next item of business. Four Tribunes from the north of France—Nâdiya of Champagne, Mathilde of Normandy, Gisèle of Maine and Fleurette of Picardy—jointly brought a proposal about the Estates General.

In 1302 the Estates General began as a small assembly of Lords and Bishops. By the 16th Century the three levels had evolved—the First Estate (clergy), Second Estate (the nobility), and Third Estate (commoners).

Tribune Nâdiya moved that the Third Estate be elected by the people and not appointed by the nobility.

Queen Marguerite stood up to ask to be heard.

Tribune Adéle recognized her.

"Would you please clarify for me and my humanist friends your procedure? If you fifteen Tribunes vote for this, will you go to your fifteen Colloquies for their vote? Or will you take it back to the elected Elders of the people of the bastides for their approval first?"

Parliamentarian Iseult of the Brittany said, "The proposal will go back to the Elders of the people of our local bastides. They will discuss and vote on the proposal. Their representative Teacher and Elder will carry their decision to their Colloquy."

Queen Marguerite asked further, "About how many bastides are there in France?"

Parliamentarian Iseult answered, "There are about a dozen bastides in each Colloquy. We represent 167 bastides."

"So…" Marguerite continued, "a simple majority of the fifteen Colloquies will move your proposed plebiscite forward."

"Yes."

Queen Marguerite walked to the steps of the dais. "My brother, the King is drafting a new form of government. You here today are well on the way to achieving the King's wishes."

Tribune Adéle recognized Jean Calvin, the King's lawyer.

"With the uncertainty in France, it would seem propitious to present your proposed plebiscite to King Francis as soon as possible."

Tribune Adéle recognized Gérard Roussel.

"Perhaps it's not all doom and gloom as much as Monsieur Calvin might infer," interposed Roussel. "What wonderful ladies we have here today! Have you left your men-folk at home?"

"These are the fifteen elected Tribunes," Tribune Adéle countered.

"And why might that be? Do you have the blessing of the Holy Father?"

"Our bastides have been overlooked by the Holy Father and his Bishops," Tribune Thérèse of Bearn answered. She did not know that Roussel had been approved to be Bishop of Bearn.

Queen Marguerite of Navarre held her tongue. Roussel would be Bishop over Navarre. Certainly, Roussel would insist on hearing her Confessions. "Oh the irony of it all!" she thought.

Roussel was not to be silenced. This time he directed his invective at Jean Calvin: "You should be purifying the Church of God, not destroying it!"

Calvin sat unmoved. His silence was more powerful than words to the fifteen Tribunes listening.

Tribune Thérèse of Bearn called for the vote.

"All those in favor of the proposal raise your hands," said Tribune Adéle.

"Those opposed?"

"I declare that the proposal has been carried unanimously. Tribunes will now take it to the 167 bastides for their discussion and approval."

Back in the Library, Calvin collected his thoughts by pouring over his translation of The Good Samaritan parable.

Marguerite slipped in. "It was quite impressive how you held your tongue through all of that."

"Your prudence was even more impressive."

She silently touched his shoulder.

"Roussel and his Papists make out the Good Samaritan to be Christ. He pours on wine mixed with oil to heal us with repentance and the promise of grace."

"So they have allegorized the Parable to suit their purposes," Marguerite responded.

"They make up a cunning story that Christ does not immediately restore health but sends us to the Church, that is the inn-keeper, to be restored gradually."

"None of this strikes me as plausible," said Marguerite. "We should have more reverence for Scripture than to allow ourselves to transfigure its sense so freely."

Calvin was livid, "Any fool can see that these speculations have been cooked up by meddlers like Rousell."

Marguerite spoke quietly but assertively, "This allegory is quite divorced from the mind of Jesus."

"So how do you interpret the Parable?" asked Brigitte who had come in with Marguerite and was listening.

"Jesus' parable does not say one thing and mean another," said Marguerite.

Calvin shrugged, "A man is beaten, robbed and left lying by the road. A priest and a Levite from the Temple pass by."

"…like Bishops today," added Marguerite.

"A lowly, despised Samaritan helps the beaten man."

"So the parable simply says what it means," Brigitte declared brightly.

"Perhaps now is not the time," Marguerite introduced her feelings, "but if you were to suggest the form of worship of Mother and Father God, how would you do it?"

Jean looked into her eyes. "It would be like the *studia humanitatis*—humanist studies. In this "renaissance" of rediscovering Seneca, or Ovid, or Jesus, you study the ancients to have something objective to bounce the present moment against."

"So you are not trying to re-institute the past," Marguerite reflected.

"Absolutely not. But you need the ancients to give you perspective in the present."

"So if we simply sit in circle and share our ignorance, we go nowhere," said Brigitte.

"A worship service should begin with readings from the Hebrew and Christian Bibles. Then the Teacher should simply interpret these readings. This is the *Liturgy of The Word*—for rabbis, for Lucian, for Jerome, for Jacques Lefevre d'Étaples. You start with reading something from the ancients—the Prophets, or Jesus," said Jean.

"This is the essence of the "rebirth" or "renaissance,"" reiterated Marguerite. "You start with an ancient model, not to copy it, but to create something new."

"The second part of a worship is where people have the opportunity to respond to the Word and its interpretation. Prayers. Marriages. Offerings. Baptisms. Social and political actions." This is traditionally called the *Liturgy of The Upper Room*."

"Explain that better," said Brigitte.

"Ancient Word and Responding to the Ancient Word in a new way," said Jean.

"Leonardo studied all the time—ancient art, ancient architecture. He carved up human corpses to understand the workings of the human body. Then, Leonardo painted, sculpted, invented…you name it," said Marguerite with great excitement.

"I watched a Gallic druidess unravel a vine that was choking a tree. Then she led the vine off in another direction. She had learned her botany and she applied what she learned," Brigitte offered. "I've watched my father study cathedral decoration and then produce something like it but newer."

A shadow crossed Jean's face, "I think Gérard Roussel puts us in danger."

"You think he is a spy for the Inquisition…"

"It would seem so…" Roussel said to me, ""You should be purifying the Church of God, not destroying it!"

"I'm also at risk," said Marguerite. "Roussel is about to be appointed Bishop in my home parish."

"That's Sorbonne politics," said Jean.

"I think you are right," said Marguerite. "So here is my plan. Roussel thinks I'm traveling south to Nerac. So tomorrow my carriage will drive off towards the south. I'll make a big thing about my 'good byes'."

Jean and Brigitte were listening carefully.

"But…my real intention is to go north to my daughter who is at Blois with her Aunt Claude and Uncle Francis. So when the carriage is out of sight, I will have my driver circle down around the hill of Angouleme to the caves."

"In the meantime, we have hiked down there…."

"I will pick you up there and take you home to Bourges."

"Thank you!"

"We can leave at sunrise."

How do you know antiquity was foolish? How do you know the present is wise? Who made it foolish? Who made it wise? Ignorance is the mother of all evils. Science without conscience is the death of the soul. I am going to seek a great perhaps; draw a curtain, the farce is played out.

—François Rabelais

...It's our salad days...

"We're back!" Brigitte surveyed the loft at Villeneuve-sur-Cher.

"It's our salad days. We're green about life itself," Jean leaned on his elbow looking at Brigitte.

"You are a great scholar with lots of knowledge. At the same time, you are so innocent…" Brigitte looked into his eyes deeply.

"Let's turn this around and look at you. You are very wise and mature in your thinking. I could talk to you endlessly," Jean followed the lines of her facial expressions.

"Let's talk about Queen Marguerite," Brigitte interposed.

"She's a strange mixture," Jean went along with her interposition. "She has a humanist piety while at the same time she is liberal."

"When I first saw you come into the Royal Hotel with her, I didn't recognize her at first. She was wearing a riding habit and hat."

"She was wearing that at the lecture earlier. I had no idea that she was the Duchess of Berry. She attracted attention as a woman equal to the men's world of the Law College."

Brigitte laughed and planted a kiss on his forehead whilst he took in her beautiful breasts.

"She is sensual like you," Jean ventured.

"You think I'm sensual?"

"In our salad days, I'm green about life itself—especially with a pretty girl like yourself."

"How long have we got?"

"That's a good question. An hour? A day? A year?"

"So let's appreciate every moment."

"Agreed."

Brigitte sat down at their little confab table. "Let's finish our project—*A Harmony of the Gospels Matthew, Mark and Luck with James and Jude*. What is the essence?"

"Jesus believed in the possibilities of humanity."

"Okay…"

"Every person is self-centered—love for our neighbor will never flourish unless one's love of God takes control," said Jean.

"So…the chief purpose of humanity is to glorify Mother Nature?"

"I wasn't going to say that. But you are right. To see God in the nature, in people, in the starry sky…"

"…and act accordingly. That is the essence," followed Brigitte. "It is also very Gallic."

"The Gaul's didn't destroy God's natural environment like the Romans did."

"The Gaul's appreciated Mother Nature," she got up and held his head to her breasts.

"Maybe we can find a home in Cisalpine Gaul," Jean mused.

"As long as we are together…"

The Teacher and his wife climbed the ladder to the loft. Iker and Xita were invited to an afternoon parley. They were among the few who could casually talk with Brigitte and Jean. Iker came originally from Spain. Xita was a Catalan gypsy. Iker met her in Barcelona where she was dancing the Flamenco.

"Welcome to our humble abode," Brigitte greeted Iker and Xita.

Jean bowed and then opened his arms wide, "This is our

...It's our salad days...

grande salon," Iker and Xita got to their feet under low hanging rafters.

"We could dance the Catalan *Rumbo* on this planked floor," Xita flashed a smile. Pillows lined the wall and floor of the intimate loft like a Bedouin tent. They sat down at a small round table set with small plates and wine glasses. A long loaf of French bread and bowl of apples sat on some colored maple leaves.

After they were seated, Iker asked, "So how are things going?"

"Between a rock and hard place," Jean see-sawed.

"I came from Spain," Iker volunteered. "My father was drafted into the Conquistador army sent to defeat the civilizations of the Novo Orbe. We never heard from him again. That's when I decided to leave."

"Iker came to Barcelona and saw me dancing," Xita laughed. "My father was a gypsy baron. He sat at the head of the table where he had the first word and the last word. My mother silently supported whatever he said. We children were to exhibit proper manners and show respect to our father. When he entered the room, we lined up like tin soldiers saluting."

"So you are like us," noted Brigitte. "The bastide covers your lives like a blanket."

"The bastide offers a camouflaged existence in the feudal world," said Iker. "The Bishop and his Medici hunting party disavow our very existence. They ride roughshod through our unadmitted community like it isn't here."

"I notice that the folk in the bastide don't strive for power and status," said Jean. "It goes without saying, these village folk were aware of us."

"You're right," said Iker, the Teacher. "Instinctively, they protect you from spying strangers."

"We four are no different from most of the bastide folk. We are all a motley mix. We are all people trying to live our lives," affirmed Xita. "In the aftermath of the bishop's hunting party, we pick up the debris."

"When things fall apart," Iker chimed in, "we put things back together again."

"Have you ever seen your parents again?" Jean asked sympathetically.

"No…"

"When my father died, I was freed of the obligation to become a priest," Jean volunteered. "I am free to live my life as a humanist lawyer."

"What about you, Brigitte?" Xita asked.

"My mother and father are both compagnons with artistic skills. My mother stains glass," Brigitte pointed to the one window in the stable loft. "My father sculpts decorative stonework. They taught me to read and write and draw. They told me stories. When we went on long walks, they identified the rocks, the plants, the trees, and the flowers."

"You are the envy of us all," Iker said.

"Let's dance," brightened Brigitte. "A gavotte for four…"

"What's a gavotte?"

"A French peasant dance. The gavotte comes from the Pays de Gap region of the Alps. Some say it's from Navarre."

"It's 4/4 time—not a waltz."

They took hold of hands and danced away the evening. Their singing provided the accompaniment.

They had a year together at Villeneuve-sur-Cher before their hide-away was exposed. The aunt and uncle of Gérard Roussel visited friends in the bastide. They poked around the market together. Quite by chance, Calvin came down to give his pony a morning run and their village host said more than he should… Gossip travels quickly especially in the Confessional of a nosey priest.

...It's our salad days...

Before the knock on the door came, Brigitte and Jean were off on their two white ponies. All their worldly belongings were in their saddlebags. To their surprise, Iker and Xita caught up with them on two white Camargue ponies.

"We liked your ponies so much…we got two of our own," Iker shrugged his shoulders. He patted his fat saddlebags. "We are going along with you."

"Let's trek the Valley of the Creuse," Brigitte suggested. "Marguerite took us there on our way to Angoulême."

"I've never gone that way," said Jean.

"Marguerite thinks it is the most beautiful valley in France."

"We've enjoyed a beautiful moment in history with Marguerite."

Brigitte looked long at Jean as they rode down into the Valley of the Creuse and began their meandering journey along its banks. Finally, she said, "From that first evening at the hotel until now, she has been our friend."

"She sees us all leaving France—all her humanist friends. She has even written a book pleading with the Inquisition for tolerance of humanists."

"Tolerance…that is the issue," echoed Xita.

"Let's visit Périgueux on our route south," suggested Iker. "It's the northernmost perimeter of Moorish influence."

"Périgueux has a Byzantine-looking cathedral," said Jean.

"I may have some Moorish blood," added Xita. "Gypsies get around."

Pseaulme quatorziesme – 14 lyricized by Clément Marot

Le fol maling en son cueur dict, et croyt,
Que Dieu n'est point: et corrompt, et renverse
Ses meurs, sa vie, horribles faicts exerce:
Pas un tout seul ne faict rien bon ne droict.

Dieu du hault ciel a regardé icy
Sur les humains, avecques diligence,
S'il en verroit quelcun d'intelligence,
Qui d'invocquer la divine mercy.

The fool says in his heart, "There is no God."
They are corrupt. They do abominable deeds.
There is none that does good.
The Lord looks down from heaven upon the children of men,
To see if there are any that act wisely, that seek after God.

...humanists gather at Nerac...

Jacques Lefèvre d'Étaples was pulling weeds in the flowers around a fountain. He was really agile for his four score years. Miles and miles of walking the length and breadth of Europe kept him in top physical form.

Stairs on both sides of the fountain led up to a courtyard in front of the chateau. At the lower level, a stone bench beckoned. When Jacques sat down, he looked across the high bridge over the River Baise and saw strangers arriving in the distance on horseback.

As the four crossed the bridge far above the river, they had a splendid view of the setting of Chateau Nerac.

Dressed in the overalls of a gardener, Jacques Lefèvre d'Étaples rose from his seat and greeted the arriving newcomers. They dismounted and tied their ponies to the hitching rail.

"Have a seat," Lefevre beckoned them to the stone benches by the fountain. "The lion won't bite," he said referring to the gargoyle spewing a steady stream of water into the basin. "I'm Jacques Lefevre," he extended his hands.

"My name is Jean Calvin. I'm honored to meet you. These are my friends—Brigitte, Xita and Iker."

"You've heard of me?" Lefevre laughed shyly without pretense.

"I've studied and constantly referred to your Classic texts," said Jean Calvin.

"And all of us have read parts of your French Bible," said Brigitte.

The textus receptus in Hebrew and Greek was the great achievement of Jacques Lefèvre d'Étaples. He had traced textual fragments back to Jerome, and from him back to Lucian of Antioch. They were keenly conscious of his scholarship in science, mathematics, physics, and politics. Then there were his five Latin versions of the Psalms and Latin commentaries on the Gospels. And recently at Antwerp, he had translated the whole Bible into vernacular French. The four were confronting the giant mind of the French Renaissance.

"Please, sit down and have a drink of water."

They drank insatiably.

"You were really thirsty," Lefevre chuckled.

"I didn't realize how much," said Iker.

"Have you trekked far?"

"We lodged last night in Lavardac. Yesterday we crossed the Garonne at Tonneins."

"Well, that's a short jaunt this morning. You're here bright and early."

"We followed the path along the River Baisse," said Jean.

"The sky, the morning sun on the waters, the meadow flowers, the chirping birds and scampering small animals—the scene was idyllic," commented Brigitte.

"All that in a dozen Roman miles! You're really quite observant."

"I didn't mean to get carried away," she blushed.

"Not at all. One comes to have a reverence for life."

"I have read some of your work on the Parables," said Jacques to Jean Calvin. "Where are you from?"

"Noyon."

"In Picardy! I'm from Étaples in Picardy on the shores of la Manche."

Queen Marguerite came down the steps.

"Greetings my friends," she said with deep emotion.

"So you know these people?" asked Jacques.

"I have been to their village at Villeneuve-sur-Cher and treated with great hospitality. Jean has been my great help in the Paris ordeal."

"Queen Marguerite and King Francis, her brother, came to our village," Iker added.

"Iker is the Teacher of our bastide," said Xita looking at her husband.

"I'm a teacher too," said Jacques.

"I'm so elated to have my two favorite humanists—the older and the younger," Marguerite poured forth.

"A humanist am I?" Lefevre wryly replied. He looked at Calvin. "Are you a humanist?"

Calvin was caught off guard. He was totally in awe of the older man.

"Cat got your tongue, Jean?" Marguerite quipped.

"He is usually not at a loss for words!" laughed Brigitte.

Marguerite smiled cautiously. It was the perfect introduction of two overpowering minds. She knew them all. Their chance meeting with Jacques Lefèvre d'Étaples in the morning light of a gorgeous day was favorably propitious.

"I have some Moroccan coffee and a croissant," she said.

"Both thanks to our Moorish friends," noted Lefevre. "Coffee

Arabica; croissant from the crescent moon venerated in the Ancient Near East."

"Iker and I are from Spain," Xita said. "We love Coffee Arabica."

They climbed the steps. The roundabout stairways and gallery above were railed with ornate balustrades. The splendid view overlooked the fountain, the bridge, and the sprawling town beyond. A small white iron table took advantage of the panoramic setting.

When they all sat down, a chef appeared in full costume. Jean recognized him to be Bishop Guillaume Briçonnet of Meaux.

Marguerite was amused at Jean's look of shock. "It's the latest fashions, Jean. The eminent Jacques Lefèvre d'Étaples is our gardener."

Jacques thumbed his suspenders like a farmer.

"And Guillaume is our cook," Marguerite continued. "He is actually quite good in the kitchen."

Jacques guffawed, "Two days ago a spy from the Sorbonne appeared at the fountain. He was so suavely incognito and all that…"

Guillaume Briçonnet was laughing hysterically.

Jacques could hardly contain himself but he went on, "Guillaume appeared in his chef's garb with a cup of tea."

"Freshly brewed," Guillaume chirped.

"From strong young green grass leaves," explained Marguerite, getting into the story. "The perfect laxative."

By this time Jacques was leaning over the railing with laughter. "You never a saw a fellow trot back across that bridge so fast…"

Jacques, Guillaume, Marguerite and Jean had actually confronted their execution stake at the Sorbonne. All had been rescued at the last minute.

...humanists gather at Nerac...

"Green tea is a great recipe for spies," said Guillaume touching his chef's cap.

"But you should keep it under your hat," winked Jacques.

They all fell into laughter.

"Bishop John Fisher in England was after me awhile back," Jacques introduced another story. "He didn't like my exegesis of Mary of Magdala."

"How so?" asked Jean with interest.

"I distinguished between the Mary's in the texts. Bishop John Fisher asserted with certainty that there was only one. He went after me for heresy."

"That's awful!"

"Then he went after King Henry VIII of England about his marriage."

"Henry didn't take kindly to that?"

"Not at all, but Bishop John Fisher insisted…"

"And now," said Guillaume, "the Pope has made him a saint in heaven."

"I notice that you don't care much for allegory," Jacques said to Jean.

"You've seen my work?"

"Yes…"

"I suppose allegory has its place…"

"But not in Jesus' parables?"

"Not to my mind."

"Agreed—take the parable about the soils and the seed."

"Yes…" replied Jean.

"One can allegorize the soils into the seed falling on bad people, good people, hard people, people in the ditch…" Jacques went on.

"But," said Jean, "the parable is really not about the soils."

"Right," said Jacques, "the parable is about the good seed being spread everywhere."

"I really appreciate that," said Iker.

"I'm annoyed at the way the Church has allegorized the parable of the Good Samaritan," said Jean. "The Samaritan is the Christ-figure. The inn is the Church prolonging the recovery…."

"The parable is really about an outcast who does the good thing," said Jacques.

"Whilst two religious types avoid the problem," Guillaume completed the analysis.

"I'm a gypsy…" Xita entered the conversation. "My people are outcastes. This is a wonderful thing you have just said…"

Brigitte picked it up brightly, "We've been dancing the gavotte. They say it originated in Navarre."

"Absolutely," affirmed Marguerite. "Let's dance."

Jacques produced a guitar and accompanied the dancing. Tune after tune was sung and danced.

"Clément Marot is translating the 150 Hebrew Psalms into French. They need folk tunes to match his lyrics," said Marguerite.

"Marvelous," exclaimed Jacques and Guillaume.

In these last years of his life, Queen Marguerite of Navarre sheltered and protected Jacques Lefèvre d'Étaples at Nérac. One evening in the firelight, he confessed to Marguerite that the one thing he had missed in his long active life was a relationship with a woman.

Tradition has it that he died that night. He was found the next morning with a smile on his face. His humanity had been fulfilled.

Queen Marguerite traveled south on her white stallion. Xita and Iker, Brigitte and Jean followed along on their white Camargue ponies. They followed the pilgrim route—the Camino de Santiago de Compostela, a path that led eventually to the tomb of James.

At Saint Jean De Pied De Port in the Pyrenees, they lodged together in an inn overlooking the River Nive.

"I brought you here," said Marguerite, "because this is the setting for my *Heptameron*.

"Like Boccaccio's *Decameron*?" asked Iker.

"Yes. Some travelers like ourselves are caught in a flood here. Only ten people survive—five women and five men. They are trapped here at Saint Jean for ten days until a new bridge can be built."

"So this is the contextual framework for stories," Iker continued his questioning with interest.

"Yes. My stories will not be allegorical. They will be parables."

"Salut," said Jean. "I like that!"

"They will hint at stories of my own life as a woman."

"I like that," Brigitte and Xita chimed together.

"Could you summarize a story?" asked Iker.

"Very well. I'm presently composing a story about a Flemish noblewoman who travels with her husband to visit a duke at his chateau. That night the duke sneaks into her bedroom and attempts to seduce her."

"This is intriguing," said Xita.

"She retaliates and claws his face drawing blood. She screams and her old handmaid comes. The duke flees."

"So where is this going?" asked Brigitte horrified.

"The noblewoman wants revenge by exposing the duke. But her old handmaid advises against it in the manner of the patriarchal Father Law."

"Oh my," Jean held his face in his hands. "Boccaccio's male braggodocia didn't give women a second thought."

"I'm glad for that reaction," Marguerite continued. "In the morning the noblewoman and her husband take their leave. The duke sends out word that he is sick, so he does not come out to say goodbye."

"Bravo," said Jean. "As a writer you are in direct conflict with the way society confers value on women."

"By following her handmaid's advice and giving up her plan for revenge on the rapist, she accepts a patriarchal definition of her place in the sexual sphere of female and male," Marguerite said ruefully.

"My mother was like that old handmaid," said Xita. "She cowered to the will of my father. My father was an autocrat at the head of the table. He had the last word on everything. We children cringed in fear. If I had come home pregnant…"

"I think that you are centuries ahead of your time," said Iker.

"You have five women and five men as elders at Villeneuve-sur-Cher," said Marguerite. "Actually, I got that idea from you."

"Five women and five men telling stories?" probed Brigitte.

"Yes. And a woman will tell this story."

"A proverb is a short sentence based on long experience… The most difficult character in comedy is that of a fool, and he must be no simpleton who plays the part."

—Miguel de Cervantes

...Are you staying long...?

Rabelais gently knocked at the door in the late evening.
 Inside the little hut, Iolantha sat with her thoughts and quietly rocked the cradle of her newborn. Jason, her son, was fast asleep upstairs on the roof beneath the ancient stars.
 "Unbelievable…" she said when she opened the door. Her eyes gradually focused on the stranger standing before her. "Unbelievable…" she repeated softly.
 Rabelais soon discovered there was more to her comment than he had expected. When he entered the candle-lit room with its low ceiling, he almost stumbled over the cradle. Then he turned and held her by the shoulders. He searched her glistening eyes… After an endless moment she nodded…
 "Her name is Panacea," said Iolantha. "She is a cure for all difficulties."
 "After the daughter of Aesklepius the God of healing," Rabelais affirmed.
 "You were so full of wine and stories and dreams when you fell asleep beside Jason…"
 "That was two years ago…"
 "Our little tryst proved more than a beautiful dream…"

Jason awakened Rabelais when the sun was climbing in the sky above the glistening Mediterranean.

"Breakfast is ready," Jason shook his shoulders and ruffled his hair.

"Hey…look at you! You've grown tall!"

"I'm ready to search for the Golden Fleece," Jason said.

"You remember the story…"

"We're having pancakes," Jason went on. "Come down right away!"

"Good morning!" Iolantha greeted Rabelais. She was holding Panacea and flipping a pancake. "Would you like to hold your daughter?"

Rabelais was always good with the humor of life, but he was getting back some of his own medicine!

"Hello!" and he took the little girl in his arms. He gave her a christening kiss on her forehead. "Can you tell me your name?"

"My name is Panacea."

"You are a little Goddess…" he said affectionately.

"Goddess of pancakes no less," said Iolantha.

"I'm supposed to make the puns," Rabelais retaliated.

"Pancakes fix everything," said Jason. "Like you fixed my shoulder…"

"You remember that? Has your shoulder stayed fixed?"

Jason punched Rabelais in the shoulder. "How's that?" he asked.

Panacea frowned at her brother. She was already protective of Rabelais.

"Are you staying long?" Iolantha probed Rabelais searching his eyes.

"I was thinking of setting up a clinic in Empuries…"

"Right beside the statue of Aesklepius…I suppose?"

"That's where I hurt my shoulder," commented Jason.

"And that's where I fixed it," Rabelais added.

...Are you staying long...?

Panacea was playing with a kitten the romped in the morning sun.

"Have you heard about the dog that was a babysitter?" Rabelais asked.

"Whoever heard of a dog baby sitter," said Jason indignantly.

> Pussycat, I'm bringing back your kitten
> I'm a Dog fed up with baby sittin'
> > Baby kitten cried all day
> > I didn't know what to say
> And besides, I couldn't find kitten's mitten

Iolantha laughed and joined Panacea with the kitten.

Jason managed a smile, "I like your stories better..."

Rabelais made a dejected face, but then he resumed his jolly self. "Tonight's the night!"

"For what?" asked Jason.

"A story, of course..."

Iolantha smiled and looked deeply into Rabelais' twinkling eyes. "Will you be staying long?" she rephrased her question...

Like poetry where a line repeats a line for emphasis, Rabelais pulled the little family together in his arms.

"Yes..."

Pseaulme Huictiesme VIII lyricized by Clément Marot

O Nostre Dieu, et Seigneur amyable
Combien ton Nom est grand, et admirable,
Par tout ce val terrestre spacieux,
Qui ta puissance esleve sur les cieulx!

En tout se voit ta grand vertu parfaicte,
Jusqu'à la bouche aux enfants, qu'on allaicte,
Et rendz par là confuz, et abbatu
Tout ennemy, qui nie ta vertu.

Mais quand je voy, et contemple en courage
Tes cieulx, qui sont de tes doigts hault ouvrage,
Estoilles, Lune, et signes differents,
Que tu as faictz, et assis en leurs rengs.

Adonc je dy apart moy (ainsi comme
Tout esbahy) et qu'est ce que de l'homme?
D'avoir daigné de luy te souvenir,
Et de vouloir en ton soing le tenir?

O Lord, our Lord, how majestic is thy name in all
the earth
Thou whose glory above the heavens is chanted
by the mouths of babes and infants,
thou hast founded a bulwark because of thy foes,,
to still the enemy and the avenger.
When I look at the heavens, the work of thy fingers,
the moon and the stars which thou hast established;
what is man that thou art mindful of him,
and the son of man that thou dost care for him?

...due diligence to write...

The Lozère in the South of France is an area of vast open spaces and mountains with few inhabitants. The Lozère highlands source the great rivers of the Loire, the Garonne, and the Rhône.

Les Gorges du Tarn slices a deep gash into these flat plateau highlands. The grande canyon sometimes a mile deep, Les Gorge du Tarn furrows through rushing narrows, roars down cascades, and sometimes flows gently into a wider pristine lake. Narrow cuts in solid granite and sloping slate rise vertically to a sliver of the unreachable sky. Light and shadow from the elusive sun add to the dramatic effect.

When the Camelotian era of the French Renaissance peaked out, humanists fled from France. Les Gorges du Tarn was one route of flight. In earlier times, the Waldensians and the Cathars pioneered these routes of escape and sought refuge here. Now Les Gorges du Tarn was a way for fleeing humanists to elude their pursuers.

Roquefort, an Occitan word, brands a blue cheese since ancient times. Pliny and Seneca, contemporaries of Jesus, speak of Roquefort cheese. The Roquefort Caves stood at the gateway into Les Gorges du Tarn. Roquefort Cheese is made entirely from the milk of the Lacaune breed of sheep. In the prehistoric era, the side of the mountain fell down and formed caves that were perfect for aging cheese. Brigitte's parents who were Compagnons brought her here as a child when they were bolstering the cave roofs and building shelves for the cheese to age.

A Roquefort bastide of sheep farmers offered shelter to Xita and Iker, Brigitte and Jean. It was to be their last night together before they parted—Xita and Iker to return north to Villeneuve-sur-Cher, Brigitte and Jean to cross the Alps to go to Ferrara.
The bastide folk were mostly Catalan gypsies so Xita was right at home. The evening was spent singing and dancing with accompanying fiddles and accordions. Brigitte and Jean were gathering more folk tunes to take to Clément Marot in Ferrara for his lyrics to the 150 Hebrew Psalms. Needless to say, they gorged themselves on Roquefort cheese, French bread and wine that warm the heart.

The foursome rode into Les Gorge du Tarn for a short distance. The four white ponies made their sure-footed away along the waters of the gorge. Iker and Xita were so entranced by the geology of the canyon that they decided to continue with Brigitte and Jean as far as Florac before returning north.
"All our belongings are in our saddlebags," Jean lamented. "Are we making a good decision?"
"Every new beginning is hard," Brigitte responded luminously.
"Isn't this a gorgeous path along the Tarn?" Iker was exhilarated.
"Mother Nature has a way of carving something beautiful where one least expects," Xita responded enthusiastically.
"We are really happy that you decided to travel with us through Les Gorge du Tarn," emoted Brigitte brightly.
"We really are glad too!" Xita and Iker spoke simultaneously.

The sure-footed ponies sought their steps along the narrows of the Tarn. Sheer limestone ramparts often reduced the ledge to

...due diligence to write...

a single footpath. The Tarn abruptly cascaded into pristine pools. Further along the Tarn waters fell again to a foaming abyss. Now and again a solar blaze would blindside sparkling granite with a spray of rainbows in the rising mists.

They were moving east in the Cevennes of the Massif Central of the Lozère. Further east the low Chaîne des Alpilles foreshadowed the high French Alps. There they would follow Hannibal's route over the top and down into Italy.

Approaching Florac, they almost missed a walking bridge over the troubled waters of the Tarn.

"Jean, stop!" Brigitte shouted from her pony following behind. "There was a bridge…"

Jean edged his pony backwards to a point where they could survey the crossing.

"It looks strong enough," Iker said dismounting.

"Let's walk our ponies across," suggested Xita.

The roaring sound of the *chute d'eau* added a fearsome aspect the falling waters into the foaming whirlpool far beneath them.

"Maybe we shouldn't have done this," Jean yowled—halfway across.

"Just keep going," Brigitte cried out.

"Don't look down," shouted Iker.

Their adventure turned out happily when the reached the other side. A petíte bastide nestled low in Les Gorges du Tarn. A few huts surrounded an inn with a beckoning lamp. The signpost read "Auberge du Soleil"—perhaps the only place in the hamlet that occasionally glimpsed the sun. A blond, blue-eyed hostess met them at the door.

"Do you have rooms and a stable for our ponies?"

"We do indeed. I'm Antoinette and this is Gilles my husband."

Jean and Iker followed Gilles to the stable with the ponies.

The stable turned out to be a barn facing on a little meadow by the Tarn. Enclosed by the river, a sheer cliff and a simple split rail fence, it was ideal for their ponies to feed, exercise and sleep.

"I'll show you the rooms." Antoinette said to Brigitte and Xita. They climbed a wooden circular stair to rooms above the pub restaurant. Bedroom suites with a windowed sitting alcoves looked down the footbridge above the effervescent falling waters.

"This is breathtaking," Brigitte said—awed by the view.

"It's magnificent," Xita exclaimed. Antoinette, their hostess was warming to Brigitte and Xita. "How long will you be staying?"

"Perhaps Jean and I could winter here before crossing the Alps?"

"You are refugees…" Antoinette measured her words.

"In a way," Brigitte examined her expression.

"Iker and I are turning north at Florac. But winter is coming. We may stay and winter with Brigitte and Jean."

Antoinette crossed the room and took her guests' hands. "Don't be fearful," she said, "My people have been sojourners for generations. That's why I like this place of refuge. Let's go back down. I have some goulash soup with veal and vegetables…"

The three men came into the pub and moved to the table where the women were sitting. Iker and Jean sat down.

Gilles bowed slightly and said, "Bienvenue à Florac-sur-Tarn. Our little hamlet is just a couple of miles from Ville-du-Florac."

"You have a marvelous setting here in the Gorges," said Iker.

"Wait till you see the rooms," Xita and Brigitte blurted out.

"The stable is ideal for our ponies," said Jean.

"And there's a little meadow where they can graze and romp," added Iker.

"Would you like some hot goulash," injected Antoinette.

"Thank you," they all responded.

...due diligence to write...

"Coming through the Gorges and crossing our rickety bridge, you must be famished," Gilles declared.

"If you want to post a letter, we have a courier who rides through once a week," Antoinette added as they spooned their soup.

"We will certainly write some notes," they all nodded.

"Antoinette, you have beautiful blond hair and blue eyes," said Xita. "But you said that you came from Tunisia?"

"We came about thirty years ago. Our family tradition has it that my grandmother several generations back came from Germany in the Children's Crusade. Instead of going to the Holy Land, the children were sold into slavery in Tunisia."

Iker cleared his throat, "On a more positive note, you make marvelous goulash!"

With their saddlebags nestled in the corner, Brigitte and Jean sat at the small pine table in the window alcove.

"Look, it's like a writing desk," said Brigitte. "It has drawers with paper and quills."

"On both sides," said Jean. "A writing table for two…and a bed."

"Shall we find out if the bed is comfortable?"

"Let's."

One day in the pub, Iker and Jean were having a beer that Gilles brewed.

"As a Teacher, I'm something of an agnostic," said Iker. "I favor life, but I'm agnostic what form it should take."

"I agree with you," affirmed Jean after another sip. "I'm dubious about people who have absolute certainty."

"You study the Scriptures?"

"Yes, but like you teach grammar and spelling and syntax."

"Explain."

"It's always good when you can compare something."
"To be objective."
"So let's distill the two similar Gospels—*Matthew* and *Luke*."
"I'm following."
"Remove the stuff the later bishops cooked up."
"Like what?"
"Like the birth stories of Jesus."
"Aren't they the same?"
"Not at all. Luke is in a barn at Bethlehem with shepherds. Matthew is in Jerusalem a week later Persian Zoroastrian astrologers."
"What about the death stories?"
"There are a dozen variations on that. The bishops really cooked up Paradise myths to peddle to ignorant peasants for profit."
"You say 'cooked up' a lot."
"A credible humanist scholar looks for what is NOT cooked up later. The bishops edited and published their cooked up New Testament in 397 at the Council of Carthage in Tunisia."
"Four centuries after Jesus lived they could cook up a lot of stuff."
"I'm 'agnostic' about the cooked up stuff," said Jean. "But as a humanist scholar I'm interested in the comparable good stuff in Matthew and Luke."
"The teachings in the Sermon on the Mount for starters. Then there are his Parables."
"When you want to discover the real Jesus, this is where you look!"
"Yes."
"I teach students the same way you talk," said Iker. "You get them to ask questions. You have them sort things out."
"I think people should learn to think for themselves."
"If you distill Jesus to the Sermon on the Mount and the

Parables, Jesus is a 'humanist'. He cares about people facing daily life in a difficult world."

"Jesus reckons with evil without demonizing someone."

"What do Matthew and Luke have in common?"

"Life, here and now. Blessed are the merciful. Blessed are the peacemakers,"

> 1 December 1534
>
> Dearest and Most Respected Queen Marg:
>
> What a wonderful fortnight we spent at Nerac followed by the trip to the Pyrenees. We loved the songs and dances, the poetry and drama, and especially the conversations with Jacques Lefevre d'Étaples.
>
> Our trek through Les Gorges du Tarn was breathtaking at every turn. We found an inn on the Tarn this side of Florac where we plan to spend the winter with Iker and Xita before crossing the Alps. Our hosts are Antoinette and Gilles. She makes wonderful goulash.
>
> Brigitte and Jean

Deep in the Gorges du Tarn, the winter passed quickly. With hay and grain, their ponies put on weight. Together Jean and Brigitte sorted their *Harmony of The Gospels of Matthew and Luke*.

In the evenings by the fireside, they sang French, Catalan and Spanish tunes. As with Boccaccio and Marguerite, each was assigned to tell as story on succeeding evenings. Brigitte kept track of the tunes for the Psalter that Clément Marot with his Dutch and Scottish lyricists were creating in Ferrara.

Later, outside in the starlight, Jean held Brigitte and looked up, "There is a certain serendipity to our finding this place of refuge…"

"The Mother and Father Gods are here in nature and in these people," Brigitte reflected from her Gallic heritage.

The moonlight was bright, so they took a walk around the meadow. Their white ponies scampered around happy to be free. Gilles had put a block of rock salt in a box. The ponies often paused to take a lick.

"I think my mare is going to foal," Brigitte said observing the animals.

Without thinking, Jean innocently asked, "Why would that be?"

Brigitte turned in his arms and looked teasingly into his eyes. She repeated his words, "Just why would that be?"

"You have a way of unloading my mental baggage," Jean laughed.

"You don't need a priest muttering Latin mumbo jumbo to create new life," smiled Brigitte.

"Our ponies did what comes naturally."

"Bingo, bango, bongo—things happen."

> 1 April 1535
>
> Dearest Brigitte and Jean, Xita and Iker
>
> What a pleasure it was to hear from you by courier.
>
> Louis du Tillet and I would like to join you enroute to Ferrara. In June, Suleiman I the Magnificent, Sultan of the Ottoman Empire, has invited me to meet with him in Venice. Francis and I met him once before in the Netherlands.
>
> Guy and Luc will take my carriage from Millau to Turin via the Mediterranean shoreline. In the meantime, Louis and I accompanied by Heléne and Jean Pierre will travel on horseback. The track way would not accommodate a carriage. We'll find your inn near Florac.
>
> With kindest regards, Marg

...due diligence to write...

That night as they gathered by the fire for songs and another story, Jean read the letter from Queen Marguerite aloud to the group.

"The Queen is coming here?" Antoinette shrieked. "That's four more people. We need at least three more rooms ready! But a room suitable for a queen!"

Gilles got the picture. The next morning he brought in local compagnons to help him strengthen the bridge. Gilles could visualize Queen Marguerite riding a powerful horse across his rickety walking bridge. By afternoon, the bridge was restored like new. The rejuvenated railings gave a sense of security above the thrashing and churning Tarn waters far below. Iker and Jean tiptoed to the center of the bridge and looked down.

The bridge rebuilding was hardly finished when Queen Marguerite actually dismounted on the far side. Recognizing Jean, Lassie, her Border collie ventured out to greet him.

"I'll go first," offered Jean Pierre.

"No. I will lead my steed across first," asserted Queen Marguerite dressed in a strikingly new equestrian habit.

"Let's go across one at a time," Jean Pierre cautioned Heléne and Louis du Tillet.

From the meadow in front of the inn, Brigitte, Xita, and Antoinette followed the progress of Queen Marguerite, magisterially coming across Gilles' newly restored bridge.

"Your bridge," Iker joked to the serious Gilles, "your bridge is truly fit for a Queen!" Gilles gave him an awe-struck glance and then was off to open the gate to the stables.

"What a marvelous natural setting your inn has here in Les Gorge du Tarn," Queen Marguerite complimented Antoinette and Gilles. They were speechless but they bowed profusely.

"I've heard about your goulash," Marguerite took the edge off things. "I'm famished."

That evening by the fireside with Queen Marguerite, Louis du Tillet, Heléne and Jean Pierre, they sang and danced French, Catalan and Spanish tunes.

"We have kept your tradition," related Jean.

"And what tradition is that?" asked Marguerite.

"Your Heptameron tradition. Each of us has told a story on succeeding evenings during the winter."

"We need to hear your latest story," Iker asserted.

"It's a very personal story. How does memory shape our storytelling? How much of our memory is constructed by our dreams and our imagination?"

"You are a very powerfully driven person," Louis said quietly yet with great strength of mind, "By your actions we here have been included in a 'renaissance' of France. We find your memory of things constructed in your imagination vital to our own self-understanding."

"Some of my poetry is very spiritual as in the eulogy to my mother, Louise of Savoy. But like Boccaccio, my preference is the discovery of folk tales from ordinary people."

"Bravo," said Iker. "Jean and Brigitte have been distilling *Matthew* and *Luke* only to discover that Jesus' preference was for parables from the lives of ordinary people."

Gilles laughed, "Jean doesn't like the stuff 'cooked up' by bishops centuries after the fact."

> "Emperor Charles V and I, when we were teenagers, were very infatuated with each other. We were possessed by unreasoning passion. Charles couldn't keep his hands off me. And, I didn't protest too much. Charles was born in Flemish Ghent in the Habsburg Netherlands. His mother tongue was French

like a Picardie accent similar to Jean and Jacques. Our trysts at Chantilly and Roberval had no language barriers. We were both French. I think he captured Francis and took him to Spain so that I would have to retrieve him. We had a love dalliance at Alcazar before Francis even knew I was there. Charles and I would have made a different kind of history. I would have been Queen of the largest empire the world has ever seen..."

My mother, the regent, could not have such an entangling alliance. She doted on her boy François. She sent him off to Milan where he won his one and only battle against Charles. My mother couldn't have me married to Charles. She fully expected her François to be Holy Roman Emperor.

I also had a brief love affair with Henry VIII in England. He had lots of Guinevere's like me. He fancied himself Lancelot because of his sexual prowess. He 'lanced-a-lot'. Henry was in no way dysfunctional. When his codpiece was off, his 'lance' was ready! Like a bull, he 'lanced' six wives. We have Elizabeth to show for it. Anne Boleyn was my dear friend. Anne was Claude's maid of honor when she married my brother.

So, for political expedience, my mother neat and tidied my marriage to a noble nobody—the unlettered Duke of Alençon! A vain chap in the local Old Boys' Club, the Duke socialized with other blue bloods about their exploits of women. These well-healed bullies bragged about raping servant girls. The Duke bragged about me as 'his doll with violet-blue eyes'.

I must say though that the Duke's personal performance in bed left a lot to be desired. Between the sheets he was not 'up to the task' if you gather my meaning. Despite boasting to his cronies, he was never able to consummate his marriage with me. With my Title, Duchess of Alençon, I carried on at the royal court assisting my mother and brother. My Duke died with his 'old chaps'.

My second husband, Henry II of Navarre was with my brother, Francis at the Battle of Pavia on 24 February 1525. They were both captured by Charles V—my first love. After I secured their release, Francis helped Henry to maintain control of French Navarre. In 1526, Henry and I were married. We had two children. Jeanne was born on 16 November 1528. Jean, born on 7 July 1530, only lived until Christmas Day…

Accompanied by guitar, Gilles sang a Catalonian love song—*T'estimo*. And then they danced a gavotte.

One by one the little group walked their horses across the bridge over the Tarn ravine. Antoinette and Gilles watched them mount up on the other side. Then, tall in the saddle, the equestrian queen led her humanist friends away on a journey through time…

As they disappeared in the mist, Antoinette looked at Gilles. "Was it all a dream that we made up in our imagination?" she asked.

Thomson Books

Other Books by Gary Arthur Thomson

First Market: The Genesis of Wall Street in Ancient Iraq
First Writers: The Sumerians
Habiru: The Rise of Early Israel
Parables on Point: Meeting The Mind of Jesus
Gretel: How The Renaissance Began
Ring Papa Ring: The Story of An American Family
Naomi: The Woman Who Knew

Books by Jeanette Kroese Thomson

Learning Together With Children
Thinking Together With Children
Once Upon A Rock
Once Upon A Rock in Doggerland
Once Upon A Rock in Yoho
Hurry Up Joey! It's Time to Go!
Grandpa Wally's Tale About His Tail

Our Website: iOriginsBooks.com

Made in the USA
Middletown, DE
01 September 2019